THE PATHFINDER
Women of the Wilderness, Book 1
by
Florence Witkop

Dear Reader:

This is a book about finding love in a small town. My hero and heroine are normal, well-adjusted people. Nice, every-day people who aren't looking for love or adventure but find them both in a small town in northern Minnesota.

The following tells a bit about *The Pathfinder*, the first of the Wilderness Women series. When you finish reading this book, if you'll take the time to post a review on Amazon, I'll be forever grateful! Just go to Amazon, type in The Pathfinder by Florence Witkop, and follow the prompts to post your review.

Now, here's what *The Pathfinder* is about:

How long can a toddler lost in the wilderness survive once the temperature drops below freezing? How can a normally sedentary woman convince searchers that she—and she alone—find the child before it's too late?

Anna Reilly grew up in the wilderness and knows it like the back of her hand but she's away when three-year-old Bobby Deal goes missing and search parties are formed and, when she returns, she's relegated to pouring coffee and handing out donuts. But she knows how to find the missing child if she can only get past the guards keeping throngs away from the forest lest they, too, become lost and make things worse. If only, somehow, she can get into the forest and start looking. She is determined to do her best to save Bobby's life and can do so by joining forces with Max Colton, her childhood friend who's stood up for her for so many years that she doesn't feel right asking for still more help.

So now you know a bit about *The Pathfinder*. If you'd like to learn more about my journey as a writer, about the books and short stories I've authored, or learn my thoughts on writing fiction, check out my website at http://www.FlorenceWitkop.com

Thanks for downloading *The Pathfinder* and blessings to you all,

Florence Witkop

THE PATHFINDER

PROLOGUE

The butterfly that was inspecting the border between the forest and the beach was all the colors of the rainbow and larger than any in the yard at home. Maybe because it was a forest butterfly? He'd never seen a forest butterfly before.

Were forest butterflies different than other butterflies? Bigger? Prettier? Or perhaps they were poisonous and if he touched this one he'd die. Bobby wished he knew.

The butterfly moved a bit closer to the canopy of green that was the forest. A foot or two. Bobby could be in that forest in just five steps if he followed the butterfly, and then he could play with it if it wasn't dangerous. But, of course, he wouldn't go into the forest because he'd been told not to, and he was an obedient child. Usually, anyway.

He scowled as the butterfly left the trees and fluttered near enough to him that he could touch it if he dared. He wished someone would tell him about forest butterflies.

But everyone—the whole family, including aunts and uncles-- were yards away on the beach, toes dug into the warm sand and wearing sunglasses as they wiggled to find even more comfortable ways to soak up the unusually warm spring day, that heat being the reason for this impromptu camping trip with so many relatives, to take advantage of the unseasonably warm weather before summer crowds swarmed the beaches and took all the good camping spots.

Bobby found the whole beach thing boring. Butterflies, on the other hand, weren't boring. If he knew about this particular butterfly, he'd talk to it. Maybe it would land on his outstretched hand. If it wasn't poisonous.

It didn't act mean. He held very still, and it came close to investigate. Then it left, but it didn't go far. Instead, it fluttered around and around and around, circling him until he was dizzy from trying to keep track of its flight.

He decided that it wasn't dangerous. It couldn't be. If it wanted to kill him it would have done so by now, and instead, it was just flying around as if wanting to be friends. Did it want to be his friend? Could that be what it was trying to say?

Suddenly it moved away, dipping and swirling through the air while heading slowly but surely towards the trees. The forest. The canopy of green that he'd been told to stay away from because little boys could get lost there.

In the blink of an eye it moved from sunshine into shadow and then continued on towards a patch of sunlight Bobby could see through the trees, a circle of shining summer warmth that was in the forest but close enough to the beach that he couldn't possibly get lost if he followed the butterfly there.

Did the butterfly live in that circle of sunlight, maybe with a whole family of butterflies? If he disobeyed his family, if he followed the butterfly, he'd be safe because he could see the beach, and he'd be there and back before anyone missed him.

So, checking to see if anyone was watching who'd tell him to stay close, he stepped into the forest.

A half hour later, the first search party was organized, just family, but they were soon joined by other campers who'd also taken advantage of the warm spring day to visit the lakes and woods and who realized that something was wrong when they saw anxious people beating the bushes and calling Bobby's name.

Not much later, professional searchers were called in, so that before night fell an intensive effort to find Bobby Deal could be organized. Reporters showed up with cameras and microphones to record the search for the little lost boy.

Next calls went out for volunteers, as many as possible because time was of the essence, and soon cars and pickups and SUVs filled with people in clothes suitable for tramping through the woods began arriving.

They'd dropped whatever they'd been doing and came immediately because, though it was warm now, a cold front was approaching that would soon change to more seasonable temperatures and, once the temperature dropped to freezing, the chance of finding Bobby Deal alive dropped accordingly, and that would happen as soon as the sun disappeared. Finding him soon was imperative.

Bobby's family fought panic, telling each other that he'd be found in time. Before night fall. Before the temperature dropped. But as the hours passed, their panic became more and more obvious.

CHAPTER 1

I liked the feel of wind on my face and didn't mind it blowing my hair every which way, even when it blew in my eyes and almost blinded me, so, after a winter of keeping car windows closed to keep warmth inside, I opened them now and reveled in every last blast of the unseasonably warm spring air.

"Like that, Casey?" He was hanging out the window, way out, and I was glad I'd made sure the windows weren't open enough for my aging yellow lab to fall through in his haste to enjoy that same wind.

He answered because he always kept up his part of a conversation. "Woof."

As the fields and towns between Minneapolis, where I'd spent the last few days visiting family and stocking up on everything that was on sale at nearby discount stores, such stores being the one thing the wilderness lacked -- as those fields were replaced by larger and still larger patches of forest and those small, subsistence farms that had been painstakingly hewed from the woods, I was glad once again for living in the wilderness. My heartbeat slowed, and my deep breathing increased, taking in the intoxicating scents of early spring wildflowers mixed with the occasional touch of snow clinging to north-facing slopes that in some years stayed until June.

Though, as for that, the truly warm weather was quickly thawing those last fingers of snow. By the time I reached home there might be none left, though I hadn't paid attention to the forecast. The temperature could drop again, one last cold snap before true warm weather began.

"Almost home, Casey."

His answer, once again, was a loud and resounding, "Woof."

I'd made peace with the fact that I'd never get rich living so far from the cities where all the high-paying jobs were located, but the trade-off was the forest I knew like the back of my hand and the lakes that were scattered though-out those forests like dew on grass. And, as I reminded myself every summer as I waded through throngs of tourists to get something—anything-- I needed in town, I lived every day in the very place where those tourists were spending large chunks of their incomes to visit, while I, in my tiny but comfortable rented house in the middle of town—all few blocks of it—could simply walk out my back door, stroll a bit, and be surrounded by hundred-year-old evergreens.

"Want to go for a walk when we get home?"

His 'woof' was doubly loud because he'd been confined to houses and back yards for days and couldn't wait to get out and run free.

I'd spent so much time in those woods growing up that sometimes I thought I knew each and every tree by name. I did know the bogs and ponds and lakes and rivers and the occasional huge boulder that unaccountably rose from the ground, and I also knew those places of tangled brush that tore your clothes and skin unless you knew how to slide through them safely. I knew how.

I knew a lot about the forest, and that beloved wilderness was why I still lived in Johns Falls after most of my high school classmates had left. I'd even opted for an online college degree that I could pursue from home, and I'd never missed the social aspects of a bricks and mortar school. Huh! Who cared about parties and study groups and walking across a campus when the temperature was below zero and I could do my homework in the comfort of my living room? Not me!

I slowed, turned off the highway, and headed towards Johns Falls. Slowed still more to deal with the traffic. Frowned. Looked at Casey. "It's not summer yet, but you'd think so by the number of cars."

Casey shook his head. He didn't know why there were so many cars any more than I did, but he looked with interest at the gathering of vehicles in the field on the edge of town.

"They are at the campground." Casey listened patiently as I thought. The campground had been there forever on the shore of the lake where I'd learned to swim along with everyone else I knew. "But it's too early for that many campers no matter how nice the weather is."

I looked further, narrowing my eyes. "Those vans look like they are from TV stations."

Still further, studying everything very carefully this time, sorting out what I saw. "Those tents—"

"No! Please, God, don't let it be!" I drew in my

breath as the import of what I saw hit like a ton of bricks, chasing away the peace of the last hundred miles and replacing it with something akin to horror. "It's a search party."

The forest could be an unforgiving place to those not as familiar with it as I was. I tamped on the brakes and wheeled into the field, telling Casey to stay in the car while jumping out and running to the tent that seemed to be where things were being organized. A man stood in the center talking to several people around him.

"What's going on?" They turned and stared at me as if I was an idiot, which I probably was, but I'd not had the radio on for the entire trip home, preferring to enjoy the ambiance of the day. "I saw the cars. Is someone lost?"

"A little boy."

I drew in my breath sharply. A little boy was lost in the forest. "We've got to find him."

A very patient reply. "That's what we're doing, ma'am." A middle-aged man with an air of authority, he stopped long enough to acknowledge my presence. "Don't worry, we'll find him soon enough. We've got a lot of searchers out there."

"I want to help." I stepped closer. "I live here. I know the forest. Do I sign something?" I looked around for a signup sheet but saw nothing.

The middle-aged man decided he'd spent enough time with one wannabe searcher. "We have enough people in the woods, but they will be tired when they come back. We have coffee and food but not enough people to serve them." He gestured to a second tent where tables were being set up. Behind that tent grills were fired up and waves of heat rolled from them. "There. Help will be appreciated." And he turned his back on me.

"I know the forest." Annoyed, I stepped towards him. Grabbed his sleeve. Pulled him around to face me. Stuck my face in his. "Probably better than anyone out there now."

"We have enough searchers. Any more will only cause confusion. We don't want to end up having to rescue the rescuers."

"I won't get lost. I know my way around these woods."

His voice grew sharper. He'd spent enough time with me, one foolish woman. He pointed to the food tent. "There. If you want to help, they need it." And he turned away once more, this time with the kind of brush-off that said his decision was final, and if I didn't like it, I could go home.

So I did. I went home, tires screaming on the pavement to let everyone know what I thought of their plans, except, having put Casey in the kitchen with enough food and water for a long time, and after making sure his doggie door was open to let him into the fenced-in back yard, I changed into jeans and hiking boots and a long-sleeved shirt that would shed branches and weeds, and returned to the field where I'd been told I should help serve coffee.

Not likely! Not when I knew the forest as well as I did. Rather, I'd simply ignore the cook tent, find out where the missing boy had been when he wandered into the woods, and start from there. And I'd do it alone. And, more than likely, if he wasn't already found, I'd find him.

Except it didn't happen. As soon as I took one step into the forest, I was stopped by a helpful, smiling man brimming with authority. "Ma'am, we have enough people looking and they are following a grid pattern."

"I know these woods."

"But you don't know the search grid. Going out there now would mess things up." He smiled nicely – too nicely – as he carefully herded me back to the tents. "But they surely do need help serving hot coffee and food to the searchers when they return, which will be very soon." He stopped and listened a moment to a mic on his shoulder. "In fact, the first ones will be here momentarily, and they'll be hungry and thirsty." He pointed politely to the cook tent. "So if you truly want to help, there's where you can do some real good."

I gave up. Went to the cook tent. Looked around and grabbed huge Styrofoam cups of coffee as the first weary searchers arrived. Shoved coffee at them and tried not to let my resentment show.

CHAPTER 2

"Hi, Anna."

I looked up, swallowed the resentment that was building by the second, and recognized the speaker. "Max."

"Coffee's good."

"Say that again, and I'll throw it at you."

He grinned. We go way back and Max knows me and that I know the forest. "Why are you here instead of out there looking for Bobby Deal?"

"Because I arrived late, and they say they have enough people, and they won't let me past the beach."

"Dumb of them. You're the best there is."

"You know that, and I know that, but all the people in charge seem to care about is their stupid search grid." I shoved donuts at him, some of my anger dissipating as I indicated hot sandwiches at another table. "More than they care about finding a little lost child."

Then I realized something. "Where are Snow and Frost? You're never without your dogs, and they know the forest, too. They aren't bloodhounds, but I bet they'd find his scent before people would."

Max looked away, then back at me. "I don't know where they are."

"Didn't you bring them with you?" I thought of something. "Or wouldn't those ridiculous organizers let you bring two of the best dogs in the area into the forest with you?"

"They let me bring my dogs."

No dogs were beside him, though they usually were so close as to almost knock him sidewise. "So where are they?"

"In the forest." He shrugged. "Somewhere."

I considered that. "Lost?"

"They're too savvy to get lost. They know the forest."

"And they ran off, and someone made you come back before finding them." That search grid again.

He nodded, but then he brightened. "If Bobby isn't found today, then I'll be out here looking tomorrow, and once he's found, I'll go back and look for Snow and Frost." He tried for a smile and almost managed one. "If they don't come home tonight, which they probably will."

"If that happens, if you look for them, I'll help." I couldn't bring Casey because his age was against long treks through the forest. "After Bobby is found, I'll be allowed back in the forest." I didn't try to disguise my disgust with present circumstances.

Max tipped his head. "If he's not found by tomorrow morning, I'm going back, and I don't have to follow their search grid. I have permission to go my own way because I know the forest so well and because, when we started, I had two dogs that also know the forest, and someone in authority figured Snow and Frost might be able to follow Bobby's scent." His head tipped. "As far as I know, nothing has changed, and I'll still be allowed to search on my own."

"Lucky you. Lucky little boy." Because, after me, Max knew the forest better than anyone in the area.

"Come with me tomorrow, Anna, if he's not found today."

"You mean it?"

"Be here first thing in the morning." He paused and looked around at the searchers now wandering about with coffee and donuts and hot, filling sandwiches. More searchers would soon pour from the woods, and the area would become crowded with the hundreds of people who had responded to the call for help. "Wait for me in the parking lot, and be there early so no one sees you with me and sends you to the cook tent. Keep a low profile."

"I'll be here." I looked around again. "If Bobby isn't found before tomorrow, we'll find him. I know we will."

"I agree, but if he's not found tonight, it'll be more likely that we'll find his body than Bobby himself."

"It's warm."

He pointed to the sky. It was cloudless and blue and lovely, but there was something about it that said things were changing, something anyone who'd lived in the area long enough would recognize. "A cold front is coming."

I scanned the sky and, with a sinking heart, I agreed. "It is." The very sky looked cold in a way that only people familiar with the region would recognize.

His voice was low and grim. "It's supposed to drop below freezing tonight."

My breath stopped for a moment. "He's a little boy."

13

"And he was dressed for a warm, summer day."

"I hope we don't have to go tomorrow. I hope he's found today. Soon." I looked at the sky again, as if looking could keep the cold front at bay, but that didn't happen. Tiny clouds formed as I watched, scudding rapidly across the clear blue, a sure herald of colder weather and, even as we stood in that field and reveled in the heat, a cooling breeze started that made me hug myself suddenly for warmth. If I was chilly, how cold was little Bobby Deal?

At that moment a small group of people came for coffee, and I served them, feeling resentment until I realized I was serving Bobby Deal's family. They took the cups and just stood, not knowing what to do, where to go. How to help find their little lost boy.

"He loved butterflies," one of them said, then corrected himself. "He *loves* butterflies." Present tense. "We'll have to take him to the butterfly pavilion when he's found." So everyone would know the speaker expected the little boy to be found alive and well.

Another said, "When he was last at the pavilion, we had to drag him away." There was half-hearted laughter at the memory as Bobby's family pretended he was fine. Then they moved off, and someone came to relieve me, and I was able to put the coffee pot down.

Max and I left. I followed Max to Jerrys Café, and we found a table at the very back only because Jerry pulled another one out of the supply closet because we're friends and he always makes room for friends. The lost child had brought people from every corner of Minnesota to Johns Falls, and at that moment they were pretty much all in this one place, gossiping, asking for news, hoping for a miracle.

And also talking about the forest and how easy it is to get lost. Until a farmer from a couple miles out of town pointed to Max and me. "You two. You're the ones. If anyone can find the little boy, you will."

Heads turned. We looked at our coffee, at the table, at Jerry himself bringing a pot to refill our cups while strategically placing himself between us and the gawkers, but he couldn't stay there forever.

A reporter came to our table. "What's he mean? Can you find Bobby?"

Jerry answered as Max and I shrank into nothingness. "These two people know the forest better than anyone else, and Max's dogs are in those woods all the time. If Bobby Deal isn't found today, then these two are the best hope for tomorrow."

The reporter gazed out the plate window that separated Jerry's from outside. Spring was advanced enough that the days were starting to lengthen but hadn't yet become the lazy, long days of full summer when room-darkening shades were all that enabled locals to get a good night's sleep.

"It's almost dark. Too dark already to be in the woods more today." It was a question rather than a statement as if the reporter hoped she was wrong, and that there were still searchers looking for Bobby. But there weren't, and we all knew it because in the forest it was much darker than on the sidewalk beyond that window. Night had arrived in the forest long ago, and it was now full dark. "And it's growing colder."

A microphone was surreptitiously thrust in front of Max while I was shunted to one side. I understood what was happening. The reporter had been at the staging site and knew that Max had been given special status, but I was a nobody, so no matter that Jerry included me in his statement, the reporter ignored me. Thank goodness. The last thing I wanted was attention that might result in being noticed enough that I'd not make it into the forest in the morning.

Max mumbled a few words that said nothing, and the reporter gave up, disappointed, then we finished our coffee and left. In the short time in the café, the weather had cooled. Not cold, not freezing, but not the kind of weather that would lure families from warm homes to laze on beaches and walk spring trails. I shivered, not so much from the cold as from the thought that somewhere in the depths of the forest a young child was alone and without the knowledge needed to survive the coming night.

At home Casey seemed to know something was wrong. He whined softly and paced back and forth as I got out sturdy clothes for the next day. Sniffed at them, and knew they meant walks in the wilderness. Stared at me and understood when I shook my head that, no, he wouldn't be coming with me, but he accepted it because, with advancing years, his days of accompanying me into the forest were fewer and fewer.

"I wish you could come. You'd be a lot of help." His tail wagged hopefully, but he merely climbed onto the bed and circled a few times on his side before settling in for the night. And all night long, his nose poking into my body told me that he'd be with me in spirit for whatever would happen in the coming day.

CHAPTER 3

My alarm was shrill, which was good because nothing less would have brought me to wakefulness since I didn't fall asleep until long after midnight, kept awake by thoughts of Bobby Deal and by the whisper of a cold, spring wind curling around the corner of my bedroom. That sound was magnified in my mind and brought mental pictures of Bobby seeking a place out of the wind.

The huge trees of the north woods would break the worst of the wind's force, leaving still, peaceful air on the ground as the tops of those same trees bent beneath the force of high winds. And there were places to get out of the cold as well as the wind, but only if you knew where to look. Would Bobby even think of looking? Was he old enough? Smart enough? Did he know anything at all about the wilderness? Could he survive?

I rolled out of bed way before dawn, dressed in a hurry, chugged down cold meat sandwiches to keep me going for a day of exhausting physical exertion, and then stuffed more into my backpack. Added bottles of water, then milk, because, if we found him – no, don't think like that, w*hen* we found him -- he'd be thirsty, but with a stomach out of whack from not eating for a long time. Milk might stay down, and every kid likes milk.

The thermometer beyond the window had dropped below freezing during the night and was only slowly coming back up. Even with warmer temps, though, a child dressed for a summer day could suffer hypothermia. And that could mean that, even if he was versed in forest lore, the disorientation from hypothermia could chase all such knowledge from his mind.

And he'd die.

Please, God, don't let him die.

After making sure Casey would be okay alone all day, I jumped in my car in the dark and peeled rubber in my haste to reach the field where I'd agreed to meet Max. Because if little Bobby Deal was still alive, he didn't have much time.

Even before the sun was up, the field was crowded with searchers ready to head into the forest at first light. A stillness lay over the assembled crowd, a somberness directly related to the cold night. Everyone knew that, after such a night, they were more likely to find Bobby's body than Bobby himself.

In a corner, huddled for warmth and companionship, Bobby's family were the quietest of all. Exhausted from no sleep, afraid of what the day might bring, trying to keep hope alive when there was scant reason for it, they spoke little and simply watched as search parties organized themselves, wiping away tears that threatened to blur the scene.

As for Max and me, we had a plan. We strolled towards the place where Bobby had been last seen. Looked around as the sun sent fingers through the trees and daylight struggled to replace the dark. And stepped into the forest too quickly and too casually to be noticed. One moment we were on the beach, the next we were among the trees.

Once there, we stopped and looked around because Bobby had done the same thing. Stepped into the forest. Looked around. And then? What? Which direction would he have gone?

As the day came to life, and the other searchers went elsewhere because this area had been thoroughly searched the day before, sunshine penetrated here and there, bringing small, scattered patches of light to odd areas of the forest and, as that happened, the life beneath the green canopy also began to move and begin the business of the day.

A few insects buzzed. A butterfly flew past and continued on, into the forest. Where was it going? "Aren't butterflies things of light and warmth?"

"They are both," Max said to answer my question. "I don't know if they are all the same and, if not, I don't know which kind that one is." He looked at me strangely, staring after the butterfly's path. "Why?"

The butterfly's fight had brought back a memory of the previous day. "Didn't Bobby's family talk about butterflies? I seem to remember hearing them talk about his love of them while I served coffee."

Max smiled at the memory. "I think I heard them say that."

"They drank gallons of coffee and talked about Bobby." I wracked my mind for their exact words. "I'm sure they talked about butterflies. Or insects, I can't remember which, but a child might not differentiate and would love both."

"Butterflies." He'd been there too and was sure. "They talked about butterflies."

We nodded at each other as the memory returned to us both of Bobby's family speaking of his love of butterflies and how much he watched them.

"One just flew past. Think Bobby saw one too?"

Max became excited. "Right here where we are standing. Where Bobby stood yesterday."

"So where did it go?"

I was pretty sure that butterflies like warmth. Even those that live in the forest would head for sunshine this early in the year because that sunshine would mean warmth. "That butterfly wouldn't head into the woods unless it knew what it was doing. Where it was going."

Max's head nodded as his thoughts paralleled mine. "Unless it had been there before and knew another warm place in the forest."

A thrill went along my spine as I knew – absolutely knew – what had been important enough to cause Bobby to disobey orders against entering the forest. "Which is why Bobby ignored his family's warning and went into the forest. Because he saw a butterfly."

"And then followed that butterfly on its way to someplace in the forest that was warm."

"A sunny place."

"First things first." I frowned and so did Max. "We need another butterfly that we can follow."

"The one we just went that way." He pointed.

"It's gone now, but where did it come from and are there more?" If Bobby saw one, and we saw another, then surely there'd be a third. And a fourth.

I glanced back the way we'd come and saw another flying butterfly. It was large and colorful and lovely enough to attract any young child's attention. As we watched, it left the warm, sunny beach area and entered the woods exactly where Max and I had entered. It went into the chilly forest even though it surely wanted warmth, and that didn't make sense unless it was headed for another warm, sunny spot that it knew of.

I looked around, aware that Max was watching me while saying nothing. Leaving me to my thoughts. Waiting for me to figure something out. Hoping it would happen because it often did when I was in the forest because it had happened many times when we were kids, and he'd ended up with bloody noses and torn clothes for standing up for me when the other kids laughed because I said I knew the forest better than anyone else in town.

I did know the forest, and Max had accepted that fact and fought for me, and now he waited patiently as that knowledge, honed from a lifetime beneath these very trees, was processed and turned into some semblance of order.

I was pretty sure that I knew what Bobby had done because it was the only thing that made sense. If I was right, perhaps we'd find a little lost boy. Or his body.

I pointed. "Bobby went that way."

Not far from where we stood, a tiny clearing where a large tree had toppled and taken down a few smaller ones with it had created an area about the size of a pickup truck where the sun came through all the way to the ground. "It's warm there." I pointed again. "Even from here, you can see insects, including a few butterflies. Bobby wanted to see the butterflies."

"Think so?" Asked quietly, so as not to disturb my thought process.

I nodded as my surety grew. "It's the most likely scenario for a child who's normally obedient and was told not to enter the forest but did anyway." I waved towards the sunshiny space. "Look at it. It looks safe. And warm. And friendly. And close enough that he'd think it would be easy to return to the beach."

He stared a moment where I pointed, then nodded. "It does indeed." Grabbed my hand and tugged at me. "So what are we waiting for?"

He pulled me at a rapid pace towards that clearing and the warmth that, when we reached it, was a welcome change from the chill of a forest that had cooled slowly but surely over the nighttime hours as the temperature had dropped and frost had appeared everywhere.

His hand was warm, his grip tight, his friendship invaluable. When we reached the clearing, I said, "Without you, I'd be serving coffee."

I wondered how many times over the years we'd stood thus, hands clasped, as friends. Except that, as the warmth of his hand over mine penetrated along with the knowledge that he'd stood up for me forever, something more that I couldn't define but knew was vastly important hit me with the strength of an anvil. I realized that, though I'd always liked Max, I'd never appreciated him enough. Now I did, fully, at this moment when life was suddenly so precious and so fragile.

"We make a good team." I meant every word. "And the dogs, of course. We'll find them, too, after we find Bobby."

"If we don't, they know the way home." He took a deep breath and pulled me close enough to see the concern that had creased his face, added lines around his eyes, pulled down the corners of his mouth. Concern for a lost child and for the two dogs that were his family. "Right now, Bobby Deal is all that matters, and I truly believe that if anyone can find him, it's you." His hands over mine tightened and warmed me to my core.

Bobby Deal was still missing, and we were standing there telling each other how nice we were. Dumb. I pulled away and got to work.

I stood in the center of that tiny clearing and turned around several times trying to see the forest through Bobby Deal's eyes, thinking of the butterflies he loved so much. As I did, I once again saw the very butterfly that we'd followed to this clearing. It was getting nectar from a pile of yellow spring flowers that basked in that brief moment of sunshine before the sun moved on and plunged the clearing again into darkness.

The butterfly didn't return to the beach. Instead it made a couple of loops around the clearing as if getting its bearings, and then it headed deeper into the forest. Which didn't make sense. Why not head back to the beach and sunshine and warmth, or at least somewhere it would find more nectar? I squinted in the effort to see where it was going.

I saw another mini-clearing, complete with more sunshine, more yellow spring flowers, and more warmth. It wasn't far away, but I'd not have seen it if I wasn't totally familiar with the forest because that second clearing was on the other side of a tangle of brush so thick that only a butterfly – or a small child – could have gotten through. I only saw it because of a single shaft of sunlight that came through the trees like a blade of gold.

That one bright shaft was enough. "This way!"

It took Max a long few seconds to locate the mini-clearing but, when he did, he nodded fast and furiously. "We'll never get through that thick stuff."

His brow creased, and I knew what he was thinking because we'd been friends so long our minds were melded, at least when something was important, as I said, "I'll get us around the brush and exactly back to where we want to be."

Such thickets are potential traps because it's easy to become lost in a few steps trying to get around them and back on track because, without a reference point, it's hard to walk a straight line and all too easy to become hopelessly lost.

I didn't have that problem, never had. I'd always found reference points from the forest itself, had done so since the first time I stepped into it as a little girl. Trees. Rocks. Branches. Everything that grew, or fell, or simply lay on the ground, told me where I was as surely as street signs tell city people where they are. Though we'd leave the straight line the butterfly took through that thicket, I'd get us back on track once we were on the other side.

Surely enough, we reached that second tiny clearing and watched in awe as that butterfly took its fill of nectar from bright, yellow flowers that grew in the swampy ground and reflected the yellow of the sunshine. Then it disappeared.

My stomach dropped. I looked at Max. He knew what I was thinking. He scowled at the place where the butterfly disappeared, willing it back so it could lead us to Bobby Deal, but that didn't happen, and we stood in

that tiny clearing looking at nothing.
    "What now?"

CHAPTER 4

I didn't know. Discouraged, I sank onto a fallen tree and simply stared at the trees that surrounded us as Max did the same, reaching out to me, taking my hand in both of his. "We're doing great. Don't worry, we'll find him."

"But will we find him in time?" Between us was the unspoken question of whether it was already too late. If he was no longer alive there was no hurry at all.

"He likes nature. He might have learned about stuff and know what to do. Might have been taught. Might figure things out." I hoped he'd know to use leaves as a blanket. To look for a fallen tree and snuggle between the exposed roots. But I didn't know him.

I said what we were both thinking. "He's so young and from the city. He's unlikely to know stuff like that." Stuff we were learning when we were his age only because we lived next door to the forest.

Max rose, pulling me up beside him. "Then let's get going. Let's assume he's a smart kid and educated. If so, he could be out there somewhere waiting for us."

At that moment, another butterfly, smaller and less colorful than the one we'd followed so far, rose from one of those yellow flowers and prepared to exit the clearing. We held our breaths as we watched to see where it would go. Back to the beach, or farther into the forest?

Not the beach. Instead, after circling the clearing a couple of times, it headed straight into the heart of the forest. "I'll bet Bobby Deal followed a butterfly just like that one. And then another. And another. And so on."

"Where did it go?" Max squinted into the brooding darkness beneath the evergreens. "I don't see any more clearings."

Confused, we both stared and watched the butterfly carefully, but all too soon it disappeared in the shadows. Which didn't make sense. "There's another warm place. Got to be. More sun somewhere. We don't know where that sunshine is, but the butterfly knows."

"So how do we follow a butterfly that disappeared if we can't see where it might have gone?" Max was truly confused and thought – hoped -- that I'd know because, as far as he was concerned, I know everything there is to know about this forest. But I don't.

I looked at him, biting my lower lip, wishing I was the wonderful, intuitive, forest expert he thought I was. But there's a limit to my ability, and I was afraid I'd reached it. I had no idea where to go next.

Bobby Deal was out there, and if he was still alive then he didn't have much time. I had to do something – had to -- and do it now. Say something. Have an idea. Create a miracle.

Then I knew what to do. A foolish, last-ditch idea. Max stood there looking at me, waiting for our next step. I took a deep breath and said, "You go one way, and I'll go another."

"Because you don't know what to do next?" I sagged and nodded and all he said was, "Okay. Good idea. Well go separate ways and cover more ground that way." A pause, then, "Until you have an idea." Then added, "Which will happen, it always does because you're good in the forest. Really good."

On a more practical note, he asked, "When do we get together again? And how and where, because we'll be going different ways?"

I pulled two whistles from my pocket. "We use these." The old-fashioned way to keep in touch in the forest, what people did before cell towers existed, a way that's used even now where there are no towers. The sound of a whistle carries a long way. "Use it if you find something. Think of something. Anything. I'll come running."

He nodded, and looked about to decide which way to go. Shrugged that one way was as good as another and set out at an angle, away from the beach but also not in the direction the butterfly had been going when it disappeared. Rather he followed a slightly clear path because logic said someone lost might have done the same thing. He waved before stepping into the shadows, eyes dark with concern, and disappeared.

I waved back. Stayed where I was. And, instead of starting out, I closed my eyes.

It's what I did the first time I wandered into the forest as a child and got lost. When the family learned I'd been deep in the forest and got back safely, they decided I must have this marvelous inborn sense of direction that allowed me to find my way home.

And, yes, once I'd been in the forest enough, I did learn how to find my way around. But not that first time.

I'd been afraid. Scared. So very scared. But, standing in the center of one of those tiny clearings that dotted the forest, similar to the ones Max and I were following now, all those years ago, I'd done the only thing I knew to do. The thing that I did now.

I'd closed my eyes, and lifted my arms, and asked for help. I'd pleaded. I'd prayed. To God. To the forest. To anyone or anything listening. I prayed for direction. For a path to open before me that would lead me home.

Then I'd opened my eyes and knew how to get home. Somehow those few seconds were enough to know that the forest wasn't the scary, evil thing many people thought. Somehow I knew that all I had to do was open my eyes and think. I was smart. I was inventive. I could figure the way back.

It worked. One tree at a time, I retraced my steps and got home and have never been afraid or lost in the forest again. But I knew that if such a situation ever happened again – a situation in which I was helpless -- that was what I'd do. Close my eyes, say a prayer, ask for help, and wait.

Would it work a second time? Would I open my eyes and know how to find Bobby Deal?

CHAPTER 5

In the precise center of that tiny clearing, I raised my arms and closed my eyes. I felt the warmth of the sun spread over me, through me. I prayed. I pleaded. I hoped. Then I opened my eyes.

Nothing. No miracle. No sudden insight as to where Bobby Deal was located. I almost cried. Then I simply looked around because I didn't know what to do. Where to look. How to find a little lost boy. I looked up again with my eyes wide open, and saw the sun moving swiftly across the sky. It would soon pass beyond the tiny open spot, and its rays would no longer shine down and make that clearing a warm, summer paradise.

But for the moment, the golden shine remained, and I blinked in the power of those rays and looked around at the tiny clearing. And, as I looked, another butterfly flitted past directly in my vision. Then another. And another. And this time, as they headed out of the clearing, I zeroed in on them, intent on not losing sight, hoping against hope that with three of them, I'd manage to follow at least one and know where it was headed.

I succeeded. Two of the butterflies winked into nothingness as they left the bright sunlight but the third, for some unknown reason, remained in my sight line as it too, headed towards the forest, going somewhere new towards what I was sure must be still another tiny clearing that would be filled with sunshine and warmth. And, possibly, Bobby Deal would be there.

I blew on my whistle, and almost before I regained my breath, Max was by my side, which meant that he'd not gone far. Had he seen me act like an idiot? I didn't want to know. Besides, all that mattered was his question. "What now?"

"We follow that butterfly."

He located the butterfly and frowned. "We lost one earlier."

But I knew the important thing. I knew this butterfly was just one of many. "There are more. There are a lot of them. If we lose this one, we'll stop as soon as it disappears. We'll not move an inch, and we'll wait and watch for the next one to come along, and there will be another one. And then another. And another. Because as sure as I'm standing here, this is a butterfly path. A trail leading somewhere."

"To Bobby Deal?" Excitement rose in Max. "If he loves butterflies as much as his family seems to think, then he probably did the same thing. He waited and watched. If one disappeared, another came along and kept him moving in the same direction we're going."

"Once he was lost, he couldn't find his way back to the beach, so he did the only thing he could do. He followed the butterflies."

"I hope you're right. You must be. Because if he didn't do that – if he's not as big on them as his family seems to think – then we could be going in exactly the wrong direction, and all those searchers walking a grid pattern are more likely to find him than we are." Max's shoulders went up and down, and he frowned at the sky. "But who cares who finds him as long as he's found?"

He tipped his head and stared hard at that china blue sky as the sun that at that exact moment blinked out of sight behind a tallish tree and left the tiny clearing in a dimness that matched the shadows beneath the nearby forest.

As we acclimated to the dimness, the very last butterfly of the three we'd been watching took its last tour around the clearing and headed towards the trees and what we hoped would be the next leg on its journey. Towards what? Bobby? Or a dead end?

We took deep, hopeful breaths, looked hard at each other, and followed that butterfly into the depths of the forest. Into that part that had lain still and untouched by humans for more years than we cared to contemplate.

It was hard going. "It would be easier for a child," I said hopefully. "He'd be lower to the ground, it's somewhat clear down there."

"So he'd have kept going."

But it was a struggle for us. By the time we got through some of the worst of it, whatever butterfly we'd been following would be long gone, and we'd stand silently, afraid to move an inch lest we lose the butterfly trail, until another one came along. One always did, showing up just as we were about to give up in despair.

That happened several times. Each time we held our breaths until another fluttered past and told us we were on the right path. "Why didn't the searchers come here? I'd think they would, knowing how much he liked butterflies."

"I doubt if butterflies came up when they spoke to his family," Max answered. "Besides, we're going uphill. It's traditional wisdom that a lost person is more likely to go downhill than up because it's easier. So they started searching where the land slopes down from the beach."

I nodded shortly, not answering because I was short of breath because we definitely were not going the easy way. I breathed a few times and looked about for still another butterfly to lead us on. I found it, watched its path, judged direction, and headed after it, all the while knowing that we'd have to detour at times to get around thickets that the butterflies and a small child could easily get through. Each time that happened I was glad for skills honed over a lifetime that got us back on the right path. And I was glad for the forest itself, which at times seemed like a living, thinking thing that told me what I needed to know if I listened in the right way.

I moved exactly as I'd done since that first walk as a child, the walk that got me lost though I'd never told anyone because if my parents knew I'd gotten lost in the forest, they'd have forbade me to go there ever again. But even back then, after that first time, I knew I'd not get lost ever again because by the time I walked out of the woods and into my back yard on that bright summer day I knew – absolutely knew, without knowing how I knew – that I could learn enough about the forest to never be afraid of it again.

"We are reaching higher ground."

"And thicker brush." I pushed aside a tangle of branches, staring into the hardwood treetops that we now walked beneath, wishing for the relative openness of the pine forests, and then dropping my gaze again in panic lest in that brief moment I'd lose the butterfly we were following.

"I see sunlight ahead." Max grunted as he stepped where I stepped because it was easier than forging his own path. "Over that hill."

"The top of the hill is covered with trees, but yes, there's a cleared area on the other side."

"I hear water."

"A creek. The woods is filled with them."

"That's why we can see sunshine. The creek creates a break in the trees."

"And provides water, which every living thing needs including insects, and butterflies are insects. I think."

I pushed harder. Max followed, reaching around me to pull branches aside so we could move at a faster pace.

As suddenly, as when we'd stepped into that first tiny sun-filled clearing with a single butterfly fluttering around, we topped the hill and instantly walked out of the shade of the forest and onto the sunny bank of a narrow creek that originated in a spring near the top of the hill and went downhill from there, singing as it flowed.

We looked around at the numerous butterflies flitting about in the sunshine.

And gasped.

CHAPTER 6

Two dogs looked back at us, Snow and Frost, sitting peacefully but still close enough to the moving water to drink from it while far enough away to not to be in danger of falling in, all the while looking for all the world as proud as two dogs can possibly look.

Between them, secure and protected and warmed by their thick, Malamute fur, sat a small, dirty, but otherwise seemingly healthy little boy.

Max moved towards the trio. Stopped. Asked quietly, so as not to scare the child, "Are you Bobby Deal?"

A nod was his answer. Max turned to me, the enormity of this miracle clear in every angle of his face, every shadow and every sun-shiny plane. "We found him." A whisper because we weren't sure how a small child who'd just spent one of the worst nights of his life might react to two strangers coming upon him.

As I examined the threesome, I saw the clear love this child now felt for the two humongous animals that had kept him safe and warm. As we watched, still unsure how to proceed, what to say, he leaned closer to Snow and wrapped his arms around the huge dog. Snow was so large that Bobby's arms didn't make it all the way around, but that didn't stop him from pulling comfort from his protector.

Frost barked, just a quiet 'woof' towards Max, a doggy explanation of this new but important friendship with a small human that was so important that he couldn't come to Max immediately because he had a job to do, a child to protect, and as he woofed, his tail wagged as much as possible for a dog sitting on the ground. Frost, on the other hand, didn't move a muscle. Wasn't about to move. He absolutely would not leave the small boy. He knew he was Bobby's guard dog and wouldn't relinquish his responsibility until he was sure Bobby was okay.

I went closer and sat on the ground in front of the threesome with Max joining me and whispering, "We need to let people know he's found."

"No cell service here."

We examined the surrounding trees. "Maybe if I climb high enough? We're already on an elevation, the extra height might do it."

"Or might not."

Before I could move, Max rose and looked for a good climbing tree, as I gathered Bobby Deal into my arms, and he let me so long as he could still touch Snow and Frost. He needed them, needed the security they provided.

Max found a likely tree, circled it a couple of times to see the best way to the top, removed his jacket, and started climbing. I watched in concern as he tried his phone when he thought he was high enough. Shook his head, climbed higher, and tried again. Another shake of his head, and I didn't think it would work, that nothing would be tall enough to allow a cell phone to operate, when, on the third try, he waved in exultation. And spoke into his cell.

I couldn't hear what he said, he was too far away, so I turned back to Bobby and the two dogs and did what I could to make the small child more comfortable than he already was, but there didn't seem to be much that he needed because the two dogs had obviously taken good care of him.

When Max oh-so-carefully climbed back down and came close, he said quietly, also careful not to disturb a small, traumatized boy, "Help is on the way."

"It'll take forever, and the forest is so thick in so many places." There were no trails where we were, no logging roads, nothing except trees and dense brush. Getting back through that forest would be slow, difficult work and would be made more so with a small child who might need to be carried. Even with the dogs, a night in the wild had taken a toll on the small child.

"They are sending a helicopter. We'll secure Bobby in one of those baskets they use for medical emergencies, and they'll raise him up." He looked straight at Bobby. "In just a little while, you're going home."

Bobby nodded. He still hadn't spoken, hadn't said a single word. But now he did. He wrapped his arms harder around Snow and reached with a foot to include Frost in his hug. "I want my friends to come too." He leaned his head into Snow's thick, white fur. "They want to come with me. I know they do. They need me. They need to be with me."

Max and I looked at each other over Bobby's head and silently agreed that we'd deal with the dog issue when the helicopter came. Perhaps by that time he'd have forgotten about the dogs in the excitement of being reunited with his family.

For the time being, Bobby snuggled into the two Malamutes and kept talking as if released at last from the silence that must have gripped him overnight with no one to talk with. "They made the bad dogs go away." He bared his teeth in an imitation growl. "They did this. Then they ran at the bad dogs, and the bad dogs ran away."

His pride in his new friends showed in every fiber of his small frame. "I think the bad dogs wanted to hurt me, but my friends wouldn't let them."

We looked at each other over Bobby's head. Max whispered. "Coyotes?"

"Or wolves." We shivered at the thought of what might have happened to Bobby if the Malamutes hadn't been with him. Guarding him. Caring for him.

I remembered the sandwiches in my backpack. "Are you hungry, Bobby? Would you like a sandwich?"

He nodded politely. "I'm thirsty too." He pointed to the creek. "I drank like my friends, but I didn't have a cup, so I didn't get much water, and I got all wet. And cold."

I pulled out the tin cup that came with my backpack and poured some water from a flask and gave it to him. He drank it greedily and then reached for the sandwich, but I kept it from him and tore off a small corner that I then held out, whispering to Max, "Too much food too soon could bring on a reaction. A little at a time is the way to go." And to Bobby, "There will be more, and milk, but finish this first."

It must have been minutes, but seemed like only seconds, when the unmistakable sound of a helicopter broke the silence.

Bobby looked up, his eyes widening as the sound grew, coming closer and getting louder. He hugged the dogs harder. As for Frost and Snow, they held their places, one on either side of him, still protecting, still caring for this small person they'd found long before we did and had kept alive until we arrived.

Then the helicopter appeared, flashing in the bright sun, growing larger as it approached until it was a huge, black entity in the sky directly above us. Bobby was afraid of it. He leaned closer into the dogs as a long line with a basket on the bottom was dropped.

Max and I looked at each other, knowing it would be difficult if not impossible to get the small boy into the basket to be raised to that noisy, scary beast in the sky.

We tried. First Bobby screamed when we tried to separate him from the dogs. Then he screamed louder and started kicking in sheer panic as we tried to place him in the basket. More trying would be useless.

We were about to wave the pilot off when Snow moved. Went to the basket. Sniffed it for a bit and then climbed in, followed by Frost. The two dogs lay down in the basket and simply looked at Bobby and waited.

They knew what was needed, and they were doing their part. Bobby was still afraid. He licked his lips and hugged himself in the chill he now felt because his new friends had left his side. He looked at us, eyes as wide as saucers, terrified of the thing in the sky and the basket hanging from it. Then he looked at his two new, furry friends. Took a deep breath. And went to the basket.

Slowly, one leg at a time, so afraid that he was

shaking like a leaf, he climbed in. And was immediately embraced by two huge dogs who book-ended him exactly as they'd done on the creek bank. He took a deep breath, and the look he gave us said he was safer in that horrible contraption with two dogs he trusted implicitly than with us in the forest.

It took a long time to figure how to secure one small boy and two huge dogs in a basket intended for one injured person lying flat, but, with the help of some rope from Max's backpack and additional webbing thrown from the helicopter, we managed, and soon the threesome – we'd already come to think of them like that, as a threesome – were hauled slowly and carefully to the helicopter, after which the door closed, and it swung on the air for a moment, and then headed back to the field near the beach where Bobby's family, the media, and just about everyone else who didn't have to be somewhere else, was waiting.

CHAPTER 7

As the noise of the helicopter and the hurricane of the rotor wash died away, Max and I, by unspoken agreement, dropped onto a boulder and watched the creek bubble from the ground below the crest of the hill we'd so recently climbed and start its journey towards a river that, with comingled waters, would continue through the lakes and rivers of the area and eventually to the Mississippi River and the Gulf of Mexico.

But this was the only place that mattered at the moment. I looked at my hands and discovered that I too, like Bobby, was shaking. "We were lucky. We could have been wrong and not found him."

"We weren't wrong." He thought that over. "*You* weren't wrong."

"The dogs were wonderful. They saved his life."

"*You* knew where to look." He avoided looking at me, turned away and examined the sky, the trees, the place where the helicopter had disappeared, anything and everything except me. "And the odd thing is that I knew you'd know. Knew you'd find him. Because you know the forest. You know it intimately, something I've learned about you over the years."

He went silent for a moment, then continued, as if it

was difficult to say what he was thinking. "Your knowledge of the forest is uncanny. Always was uncanny. Surreal. Impossible." His voice went hoarse as he finally said what he'd undoubtedly thought more than once during our years of friendship. "It's as if you and the forest have a connection. As if you talk to one another. If I didn't know it was impossible, I'd think that you asked it where Bobby was, and it told you."

"It was the butterflies. Just the butterflies."

"I suppose so." But his voice said he wasn't sure.

I didn't know what to say. I love the forest, but to think I communicated with it as to another person? People don't talk to trees and expect them to answer, even though as I child that's what I'd thought I was doing. Until I grew up enough to know that such things don't happen, but it was also true that I'd needed a moment surrounded by the trees I love in order to figure out where Bobby might be, and that had necessitated Max being gone, and he might see that as me communing with the trees.

So now I scrambled for another topic as I'd done as a child when people asked me how I knew my way around the woods so well. And I found one. The dogs. His wonderful dogs. "If he hadn't been found until days from now, when the searchers finally realized they were looking in the wrong place and moved somewhere else, if he'd been lost all that time, the dogs would have kept him safe."

"They are heroes." A smile misted across his face as he forgot about my knowledge of the wilderness and thought instead, of his beloved dogs and what they'd done, which was save Bobby Deal's life.

"That they are." I smiled, glad of the diversion, but

also because I've always loved Snow and Frost as much as I love Casey.

Max guffawed and threw a stick in the creek, and we laughed in a sudden release of tension as it floated around the bend, bumping into rocks as it went. "And here I thought they'd just run off for some fun in the forest and would return home when they were good and ready."

He looked towards the creek instead of at me and followed a leaf that the stick had jarred loose from the bank as it, too, swirled on the current as if riding a merry-go-round, until it too disappeared around the bend. I could imagine both stick and leaf ending up on some far distant shore as, beside me, Max relaxed, finally coming to terms with what had just happened, the whole of it, including the scary and the miraculous and the sublime.

"You have no idea what I planned on telling those dogs when they finally came home. Hey, forget telling, I planned on shouting at them, screaming maybe, and my language wouldn't have been very nice."

I giggled, which meant that I, too, was finally relaxing on some deep level because Bobby Deal was alive and well and on his way to his family, but most of all because Max's dogs were responsible for his good health. Max's wonderful Malamutes. "All the while, they were busy saving a little boy's life."

He took a second stick, and I thought he'd throw it into the creek, and we'd watch as it too began a long journey elsewhere. Instead he rose, threw the stick away, and reached for me. Pulled me up beside him. And we stood there inches apart, not looking at each other but not looking away either, I found myself taking from him the same thing that Bobby Deal must have taken from the dogs as they sat on either side of him, guarding and caring for him. I took comfort. Peace. Certainty.

I also found myself leaning into Max as I was sure Bobby Deal had leaned into the dogs until I heard the beating of his heart through the sturdy fabric of his shirt and jacket and felt the rise and fall of his chest as he breathed. And I had the oddest feeling that we were becoming one person, melting into each other, breathing together, giving each other the additional warmth we needed because the early spring sun didn't quite warm us through and through.

And as I lay against his chest, not wanting to be anywhere else, I wondered, abruptly what was happening because in all the years we'd known one another I'd never done this before. Never felt this way before, not with Max, not with anyone. Never had this impulse to simply touch someone and stay that way forever, and the odd thing was that I felt that way with Max my friend and no one felt that way about a friend. Just a friend.

If anyone would have said I'd behave the way I was behaving right there, right then, I'd have laughed myself silly. But I didn't deny how I felt and didn't try to convince myself that it was just the emotionally charged situation and nothing more because, at some level I knew it was more than that, though I couldn't imagine what. Years of friendship, I finally decided.

Then I shook my head angrily against his chest and told myself I was an idiot and had been in the woods too long, after which I pulled sharply away, and we set off for home.

The trek back was a reverse of the trip to the creek except that we didn't crawl through thickets following a butterfly path. Instead, whenever we reached a particularly nasty place—and there were many of them-- we simply went around it. But, by unspoken agreement, we always returned to the butterfly path because they were lovely and we enjoyed watching them flit beneath the trees, and they went straight as an arrow from one sun-filled clearing to another until, finally, we could see the greater burst of sunshine that was the beach area.

We stopped before leaving the silence of the woods. Looked around greedily for one last fill of the canopy of solitude. Listened. Heard the sound of people moving and talking, of vehicles coming and going. Not the helicopter because it had arrived before us and possibly had already taken Bobby to wherever he needed to be to make sure he was okay. We hung back in the forest, reluctant to leave our green, protected area and once more join the everyday world, surprised at how weary we were after the search. Not physically, but emotionally, even though we'd been successful.

Eventually we looked at one another ruefully, acknowledged that the end of something eventful had finally come, and walked the few yards from the forest and onto the brightly lit beach.

And straight into mayhem.

CHAPTER 8

For a few long moments we just stood there and looked over the assembled crowd and, yes, there were a lot of people. All the searchers who had been pulled from the forest because they were no longer needed were there plus the organizers of the search, Bobby's family and of course the media, complete with vans and cameras and microphones and notebooks.

We watched in absolute amazement as we saw Bobby himself and realized that he hadn't yet been taken anywhere. Because he refused to leave Snow and Frost as in the forest? He wasn't smiling, but seemed content, surrounded by his family and still bookended by two huge Malamutes who were still in full protector mode only with tails wagging nonstop as they happily accepted pets and hugs from everyone who wanted to pet or hug them. Which was everyone.

"Couple of actors." Max snorted and grinned at the same time.

I examined the dogs and the small child between them. "I suspect that your dogs are going to be famous."

Max could only nod, dumbfounded, as Bobby looked up and around and saw us. He waved, and we waved back, and just like that all those media types and half the crowd around Bobby and the dogs swerved towards us. And then, as one, they came our way with the media people running flat out to reach us first and make us as famous as the dogs.

"Whose dogs are they?" A microphone was thrust in front of us.

I pointed to Max. "His."

I was about to say that they were Malamutes and give the reporter their names, but didn't have time because as soon as I pointed towards Max, the microphone swerved towards him, and the entire contingent of people swarmed all over him.

I was left alone. Ignored. And happy to be pushed aside, even though I felt sorry for Max and the sudden inundation of attention. But not sorry enough to save him. After all, he was the owner of hero dogs and the one who could tell the reporters what they wanted to know.

Which was everything. How old were they, what were their names, had they saved any other lives that Max knew of, did they do this sort of thing often, and how did they end up in the forest anyway? I backed away, step by step, feeling sorry for Max, but not too sorry as, over the heads of all those reporters, I waved to him and caught his wry expression that said I should run for cover while at the same time accusing me of being a coward for leaving him alone to deal with this onslaught of attention.

"Aren't you the lady who was pouring coffee yesterday?" I bumped into a man as I backed across the field. He twirled me around, laughing because everyone was laughing, smiles were epidemic with Bobby safe and sound. "The current servers are worn out. Exhausted. They could use some help." So I meandered over to the food tent, grabbed a coffee pot, and started pouring as if it was what I'd been doing all along instead of tramping through the woods.

Now that the search was successfully ended, everyone wanted to relax, have a cup of coffee and a roll, plop onto a handy chair or bench or piece of field, and tell each other about the amazing rescue and the dogs who were about to become nationally famous, maybe world famous, while, as for me, I remained happily invisible as I became just the woman with the coffee pot. And soon learned to appreciate how hard such servers worked.

I followed the events across the field as I poured coffee and listened to the gossip around me. Everyone had a story, the locals especially, because they knew Snow and Frost and were eager to give anyone and everyone whatever information about the dogs they possessed. Soon the life history of Snow and Frost were common knowledge from puppyhood through small town dogs to heroes, and we had to make more coffee and send out for more rolls even though we thankfully were able to forego meals because, as everyone talked and congratulated each other on a search well done, the tents were already being taken down, and the first cars were disappearing as their owners returned to the every-day worlds of work and family. Smiling because Bobby Deal was alive and well.

Then the helicopter warmed up, rotors whirling, chasing everyone a safe distance away, and as I watched, Bobby and his mother were lifted inside along with two huge dogs. I was pretty sure I knew why Snow and Frost were included. Because Bobby wouldn't go without them in which I was proved right when I heard a voice at my elbow.

"How about some coffee, and then you and I get out of here and find some privacy because I'm not going to see my dogs for a while." Max made sure we each had a cup and steered me by my elbow back into the forest, which was the only place not covered by throngs of people, and we found a tree and slid down its trunk and simply sat and looked back at the beach area.

The first thing Max said, after tasting his coffee and donut, was, "Don't worry, I'm not mad at you for deserting me." He stretched his body as much as possible while still leaning against the tree trunk and gave a huge sigh of relief. "I wouldn't wish what I just went through on anyone."

"What about Snow and Frost?"

"The dogs?" He snorted. "Did you see them? The beggars!" He snorted again, though it was hard because he was also laughing. "They are eating up all this attention. I never knew what a couple of hams they are. Did you see them? Smiling and nodding and acting like royalty."

"How will they get home?"

He shrugged, turned the shrug into another stretch and sighed again blissfully. "I don't know but I'm sure someone will do something. And I wish those hospital people good luck with separating Bobby from the dogs for long enough to make sure he's okay physically."

"He is okay. Because of Snow and Frost."

"And because the coyotes didn't get to him. Or wolves, whichever they were."

"Yeah. Good thing the dogs were there, and I

almost feel sorry for any wild animal that thinks those dogs are pushovers."

We subsided into silence, unable to hear the sounds of the forest because of the sounds of humanity beyond the trees, though it was just a low hum because the sound barrier of the trees was enough to blot out anything subtle.

So we sat and reminded ourselves what normal was and that we could return to it as the sun moved across the sky and could no longer penetrate the thick foliage. The forest grew darker with each passing minute until we were lost in a not-quite-real world of muted colors. Green and brown and multicolored wildflowers and the earthy scents of early spring in the northland.

Max's hand caught mine and brought it close to his solid body and then turned it over and examined it. It was grimy and with fingernails that needed trimming, but not callused like his because I'm not a physical fitness nut. When I got home, I'd jump in a tub with a ton of bubbles and soak for an hour or so. Or longer.

He kept my hand and encased it in his larger one. I let it stay because it felt right. Good. Natural. Comfortable, and something else, something I didn't remember feeling ever before during the years we'd known one another but was the same thing I'd felt in the forest and, whatever that unknown something else was, I welcomed it even as I didn't understand it. Sought it out. Greedily took it into myself and reveled in it and wondered what it was and what had changed between us. Because something had and whatever it was, it was fundamental.

As the crowds thinned in the field because Bobby Deal was no longer there, and the tents were dismantled, and there was nothing left to do, we left our green and brown sanctuary and strolled slowly to our vehicles. Climbed in and drove each to our own home.

Where I didn't take that bath after all because I was suddenly too exhausted to do more than down cold soup straight from the can and fall across the bed with Casey curled on his side and watching, clearly curious as to where I'd been, and what I'd been doing.

He spent seconds sniffing gently at the scents of Snow and Frost that were all over me because the three dogs were friends. His quiet but impolite snuffle let me know that he was a bit miffed. I'd visited his friends and not taken him along.

I murmured sleepily that there was a good reason, and he accepted my explanation, but with reservations. In the morning he'd need an extra treat. Then I fell asleep and dreamed of little lost boys, big wonderful dogs, and a man I'd known all my life and suddenly didn't know at all.

CHAPTER 9

The next morning, I took that bubble bath and spent enough time in the tub to emerge with wrinkled fingers and no dirt anywhere. Trailing a bath towel, I dropped onto my bed where I trimmed and buffed my nails and applied pale pink polish and felt once more like a female. Then I gave Casey his extra treat and was accepted back into his good graces. And I didn't do anything more until Monday when the work week began.

Work that Monday consisted of entering the spare bedroom that I'd furnished with a second-hand desk, a computer that belonged to Hollander and Company, all the things that came with a company computer, plus the pile of papers I'd brought home because I choose to work at home much of the time though I do make the occasional trip to Hollander and Company to make sure I'm still employed.

Small towns are great for jobs that don't pay much but allow for a decent, slow-paced life. I think Hollander bought the building next to Jerry's Pizza because their employees like pizza and they hoped that meant that their work-at-home employees like me would actually come to work occasionally as a stopover on our way to pizza and gossip at Jerry's.

I was thinking along the lines of pizza when I felt the breeze from a door opening. I didn't bother looking. "Hi, Max."

He came all the way in, closed the door, and asked, "Are you okay?"

"Of course. Why wouldn't I be?" I stretched like a cat because it was a beautiful day with sunshine along with the feel of the perfume of spring enveloping me that had come in through the open door. And, of course, Max was here, which was another reason to smile. Because we were friends, and visits from friends were always welcome.

I thought about my best friend for a moment and decided that Max could legitimately be described as delightful in a friend-who-is-a-good-looking male kind of way.

"Just thought I'd check and see how you're doing." He looked at me sidewise, not noticing the pink nail polish, but aware that I'd been imitating a contented cat. "After yesterday, I mean."

"Yesterday, we found a lost child. That makes me happy, so why are you asking if I'm okay?"

"Because of how you were kind of shoved aside because the real story was suddenly and unexpectedly the dogs, and they are my dogs, so I was interviewed because the dogs don't answer questions well."

"Thank you for answering questions so I didn't have to."

"That's what you say, but do you mean it? Are you sure you're not put out? Don't feel ignored? Aren't angry?"

I went close and put my hands on his shoulders while noticing not for the first time the way his muscles flexed beneath his shirt. Should I notice that about a friend? I wasn't sure.

"I am not angry. If anything, I'm eternally grateful to you for taking the heat instead of me." I could feel the solid bulk of his shoulders through the fabric of his shirt and was kind of proud that I'm friends with a guy many women would give anything to know.

I explored him further. The warmth of him, the smell of soap and water and something else, whatever it was that I'd felt the day before. I hadn't known what it was back then in the forest and here it was happening again in my kitchen and, combined with the feel of those muscles, I reacted suddenly and viscerally, a reaction that was totally unexpected, and it happened with Max, my childhood friend! I shouldn't feel like this. I dropped my hands quickly.

He was standing, watching me, waiting for my answer. "Like I said, I'm glad you were there to take the heat instead of me." I looked away and gathered my thoughts and hoped he hadn't noticed anything unusual. "If those reporters had asked me how I knew where to find Bobby, I wouldn't have known how to answer."

"You'd tell them we followed butterflies." He was puzzled. "A simple explanation because that's what we did."

"I wish it was simple." I let my gaze meet his and he felt my agitation because he knows me inside out and because, if he'd noticed anything untoward earlier, maybe I could send his ideas elsewhere. It would require telling him something I'd never told anyone before, but perhaps this was the time. "But it's not because when I said it was just the butterflies, I lied."

As for Max, he stared at me, through me, and then grabbed a couple cans of pop and took my hand and led me into the yard where we found a patch of shade and leaned against the sturdy wooden fence that kept Casey in check whenever I was gone, after which he leaned over me, blotting out the scenery, and said, "So tell me how it's not simple."

"It goes back to when I was a little kid. Really little. When I got lost in the forest."

"You were lost in the forest? You? Anna Reilly?" His eyes grew round, and I knew I had his full attention. "I'm amazed. I thought you were incapable of getting lost in the woods. You're the original pathfinder." His eyes slanted towards mine, dark and full of surprise.

He'd forgotten all about my odd reaction to his presence. Good. "I never told anyone. I was afraid my parents would go all wonky and never let me in the woods alone again."

"They'd probably have forbidden you to leave the house! But I'd think that, after being lost, you'd never want to be alone in the forest again. It's how I'd have felt."

"I didn't stay lost. That's the thing, the important thing, the thing I need you to understand, the reason I'm telling you now." And, oddly enough, it was one of the reasons. Making him forget how I'd acted was only part of why I finally spoke about my childhood experience. "If I told them what I'm about to tell you now, they wouldn't have believed me. Wouldn't believe me now. Probably would call a psychiatrist."

He chewed his lower lip. "Okay. I wouldn't let you

go into the woods if I was responsible for you and thought you'd get lost. If I'd known that you were lost. But I only know you now, and I know it's impossible for you to get lost because you've got – a thing. A feel for the lay of the land. A kindship with the forest. You don't get lost. Ever. And you can find little lost boys." He thought over what he'd just said, and a question loomed in those oh-so-dark eyes. "But why'd you wait until now to tell me? We've been friends forever. I'd never rat on you."

"You'd not rat on me, but you'd not believe what happened."

His eyes half-closed, his body language changed, morphed, and he went all still. "So tell me."

"As it turned out, I wasn't very far into the forest, not like Bobby Deal, but I was far enough that I got turned around."

"It happens. Not to you, but you were a kid, so I'll agree that maybe that once you got turned around."

"I didn't know which way to go. I was scared. So scared."

"Of course you were." I could see in his face how he'd have felt. Terrified.

"I didn't know what to do. There was no one to ask for help."

"You poor kid. You were alone."

"So I asked for help." It was hard speaking, even to Max. My chest hurt, it was hard to breathe as I told him what I'd never told anyone. "I closed my eyes, lifted up my arms, and asked—begged-- for help."

He said nothing, and I wished I'd not told him, but before I could take back my words or turn them into a joke, he asked very carefully, one word at a time and with no inflection at all to indicate what he was thinking, "What happened next?"

"The forest answered. I was little, I didn't know much about life, but I knew that someone answered." It was still hard to breathe, but easier now that I'd got it out, now that I'd said it out loud, and it sounded ridiculous, so I got the rest out in a tumble of words. "At least I thought someone did, but I was a kid, and I didn't know that forests don't talk."

"So after thinking that the forest spoke to you, you found your way home." He turned that over in his mind. "How, exactly?"

"I think that the simple act of closing my eyes and talking calmed me down enough that, when I opened my eyes, I was able to look around and see things that in my panic I'd missed earlier. You know the kinds of things I'm talking about. The way the sun falls on the trunks of those few trees it manages to shine on so as to tell me which direction was which.

"The trees themselves that were the kind that grew where I'd been walking, which were different from the trees deeper in the forest, and I knew the difference. Younger trees were closer to home and growing thickly together because there was more sunlight at the edge of the woods. Things like that. Looking back, I think that's what happened."

"You were too young to have learned stuff like that. Hey, I don't know stuff like that even now."

"Who's to know at what age people acclimate to their surroundings? Maybe that was my time."

"Maybe." He was skeptical. "Or maybe the forest really did talk to you. Or, if not the forest, some higher power. God, maybe?" The way he tilted his head said what he thought had happened. "Angels?"

I shook my head in the confusion I felt every time I'd tried to figure it out. "Any or all of those things. Or perhaps I simply grew attuned to the forest that day and have remained so ever since."

"Enough that you found a small, lost boy."

"I didn't find him. I overheard his family talk about his love for butterflies, and I followed them."

"Hummmph!" He let me know what he thought of that explanation. "However all that matters is that you found Bobby Deal and that you have the most remarkable forestry skills of anyone I know, and if I'm ever lost in the wilderness I want you to look for me because you'll find me before I even know I'm lost."

I giggled, he grinned, the moment passed, and we were once again just good friends with a lumbering yellow lab named Casey trying to climb all over us because we were sitting on the ground, and he considered that a good enough reason for a hug. Or two.

"I'm glad that we're friends, Max."

"That's us. Friends." His voice was hoarse. He cleared his throat and looked away a moment and then back at me and grinned. "Friends forever."

"You didn't laugh at my childhood story. That's true friendship." I flushed. "I mean the part where I actually thought the forest spoke to me, so I either have some kind of psychic connection to trees, or I'm a psycho."

He flushed himself and there we sat, two friends blushing like a couple of idiots. "There's a reason I didn't laugh." Coughed. "I kind of semi-believe in psychic phenomena." Sounded hoarse once again. "Sort of."

Really? "What's your story? What happened to you that you never told me about just like I never told you about getting lost?"

He stared at me, nose to nose, eyeballs to eyeballs. "Promise not to rat me out?"

I held up one hand. "I promise."

"It's the dogs. I know everyone thinks they communicate well with their dogs, but there have been times when I've thought that my connection to Snow and Frost is like – like – like your connection to the forest."

My breath went out in a whoosh. I'd never in a million years have thought rational, no-nonsense Max could think such a thing let alone admit it. "So is it real? Do you have a psychic connection to the dogs? Or just your imagination?"

"I don't have a clue."

"Me either, regarding my ability in the forest."

We stared at one another. Laughed. And put the whole thing behind us, and I asked him to stay for lunch because it was too late for breakfast, and I was starving after having spent my morning pretending to work and failing completely.

A good lunch would change all that, and I'd get a lot accomplished in the afternoon that stretched ahead warm and peaceful and waiting for all kinds of good things to happen because I'd divulged my most deeply-held secret to my best friend, and he'd not laughed and, moreover, he'd done the same to me. Which meant that we were two of a kind and, oddly, that thought made me feel better than I'd felt in a very long time.

We moved and stretched the kinks of sitting far too long out of our bodies and then prepared to rise and head for the house. And stopped, as a voice asked, "Aren't you the people who found Bobby Deal?"

CHAPTER 10

We turned and found ourselves looking up at a tall, reed-thin woman in gun-metal gray jeans and matching leather jacket that had been expensive when new and had received good care all its life but now was worn so thin that it resembled silk, and my first thought was to wonder what she'd done over the years to wear out such a tough jacket. Because she didn't look the type to wear second-hand anything. She was peering down at us from the other side of the fence, and was every bit as sweet-looking as my grandmother and just as intimidating.

She was definitely past middle age, without being old, and was wearing large, round glasses and a gray, leather cap that matched the jacket and sat at on her salt and pepper hair at a jaunty angle, with that hair held back in a clip that said she didn't have time to bother with non-essentials like hairdos when life got busy, and it was clearly busy now.

Her eyes stared at us and right on through to our backsides, seeing everything that was in the open and everything we tried to hide. They were bright gray eyes, alert and intelligent and intent on us. We looked at each other warily and wondered what we were in for now.

"Well? Cat got your tongues? Are you the heroes of the hour, or aren't you?"

Max spoke. "The heroes are the dogs Snow and Frost. I'm their owner, or to be truthful, their caretaker because they graciously allow me to live with them in my house." He deliberately turned back to me and away from the woman whose nostrils dilated in silent laughter as she gave him kudos for a good reply. Those pale eyes sparkled with appreciation.

Instead of leaving, though, she came closer and rested her hands lightly on the fence. "So you are the people who found him." She nodded to herself, muttering that she'd known who we were all along. "You're the couple who called for the helicopter." She sniffed delicately. "And yes, I'm probably the only reporter in the world who noticed that there were two rescuers instead of one."

"Reporter?"

"The free-lance type, but I'm good, so I make a decent living sniffing out the stories everyone else misses, and that's why I'm here." The hands came down harder on the fence with neatly manicured fingers splayed across the top. "For the story behind the story."

Max's eyes widened, and our looks met, and then he reluctantly turned back to acknowledge the stranger now leaning companionably on the fence while taking in the entirety of the yard with its dilapidated swing set, scraggly early spring grass with bare patches here and there, and Casey, who was sunning himself on the patio and watching her with half-closed, sleepy eyes while his tail thumped lazily.

Casey liked her. She must be a decent person. Darn. I sighed and wished otherwise because it's wrong to ignore nice people, and I definitely wanted to ignore her, as Max, bless his heart, was doing his best to push her politely away.

"The dogs aren't here, so if you want to see them, you'll have to do so some another day." He rose and wiggled his shoulders in a polite brush-off and then prepared to lead the way to the house, as I made ready to follow and shut the door firmly once we were inside. And draw the drapes. And lock the front door.

The slender woman snorted. "Don't go yet." Sniffed. "It's not polite, and I'm quite sure that both of your mothers taught you good manners."

Max paused. "There's nothing for you here, but I promise that you can see the dogs some other time."

Her eyes lit once again with appreciation for how good Max was at giving her a polite shove out of our lives. "The dogs are nice, I'll give you that, but everyone and his brother has said just about everything there is to say about the canine heroes who saved Bobby Deal's life. I'm not here because of the dogs."

Max paused halfway to the house, meeting my look as we debated whether to make a dash for the safety of the kitchen, or find out why she was still leaning on the fence in such a friendly way while saying she wasn't interested in the dogs. Everyone was interested in them. "So why are you here?"

It was in her eyes. Triumph that she'd got this far, which meant that the rest would be easy. "To meet you two." Her look left Max and rested on me, and I felt the weight of that look and her interest in a shiver that ran through me. A not unpleasant sensation, but it was odd.

I'd never been inspected quite so thoroughly before. "Actually I'm here to meet this young lady."

She gave up all pretense of talking to Max, as she switched to me. "To interview you because I believe you are the real story."

"Me?" I squeaked the single word and knew my throat wouldn't allow anything more.

"Yes you." She nodded sagely, and I saw her mind working nonstop as she calculated the effect of her words and the sound of that squeak because it meant she was right and there was more to the story of Bobby Deal's rescue than the two dogs who'd kept him warm and safe. A lot more. "I knew it! I knew you were the real story."

She vaulted over the fence and into the yard with an agility that belied her years, coming towards us and taking out a pocket-sized recorder. "Just so you know, I'm good at what I do, and I specialize on the story behind the story. My intuition has been screaming at me ever since Bobby was rescued. It's been jumping up and down and yelling and pushing me straight to you, young lady, and, as usual, it was right, and because I always listen to my gut, I suspect that I'm about to get the story of a lifetime." She pushed her cap back until it threatened to fall off, but I was sure it wouldn't dare as she came still closer. "Mind if I ask a few questions?"

At that moment Max yanked me behind him so hard that I wasn't sure my feet stayed on the ground, and we disappeared in the house, and as soon as the door slammed behind us, he made sure it was locked and then pulled the kitchen curtains closed and then sat at the kitchen table and said morosely, "I thought all that news stuff was finished."

I poured us each a cup of coffee and sat across from him. "Was this what it was like with all those reporters crowded around you?" He nodded dumbly. "Then thanks for saving me."

He placed his hands flat on the table and examined them as if wondering why they couldn't keep us safe from prying eyes and inquisitive reporters. "Maybe it never ends. Maybe it goes on forever. For the rest of our lives."

I whooped with laughter. "Not a chance. Tomorrow's story will push us aside."

"Then I wish tomorrow would come immediately, because I'm more than ready to be done with all this."

I went to the window and pushed aside the curtain enough to see the empty back yard. "She's already gone, so maybe she's given up on the Bobby Deal story and is on to the next one."

"She said she's looking for the story behind the story." He gazed at me in a kind of wonderment. "And she thinks you are it. She *knows* you are, and it's amazing how she sniffed out the truth when all those other reporters took pictures of dogs."

"I'm not a story. I just followed the butterflies."

He gazed at me pointedly. "So, if she comes back, that's what we'll tell her. That you overheard the family talking and so figured out that butterflies would lead to Bobby."

I nodded. "That should work because it's the truth. We simply followed a bunch of butterflies, and if we sound convincing enough – and boring enough – she'll decide butterflies aren't a good story, and she'll leave."

"Unless her instincts are better than good—and so far they are—and she knows that the reason you were able to follow the butterflies once you knew Bobby liked them was that you know the forest better than anyone else in the area. Better than anyone else in the world. If she figures that out, she'll be back, and if I know reporters — and I've learned a lot about them in the last day or so — she'll figure it out. Because that's what they do. What she does."

"I hope not." I wiggled uncomfortably. "Besides, you're making me out to be more than I am. I just like the forest and have been walking around in it for most of my life."

His eyes narrowed. "Without coming to harm or getting lost or any of the things that happen to most of us, even those of us who've lived here forever. Some people around here make their living from the forest and are in it all day every day, and even they don't have your uncanny ability."

"It's luck." I was downplaying what I'd told him earlier and suddenly, inexplicably, trying to convince him that I knew less about the forest than I really did. Did he buy it? Of course not because he knows me. "Nothing more, nothing less, and yes, I've been fortunate every single time I've stepped into the woods." I wished I'd never told him about my childish adventure because then this conversation might not be happening. "And please don't call the men in the white suits just because I had a huge imagination as a kid."

I was still by the window, and still holding that curtain to one side, as Max rose and joined me, and then took the curtain from my hand and let it fall, shutting out the outside world while turning me towards him. Then he simply gathered me in his arms and pulled me close. "I will never, ever call the men in white coats for you because you are the girl I've known forever, and that girl has a sensible head on her shoulders." And he pulled me still closer, and I leaned into his chest.

I already knew what he felt like. I knew the fresh-air scent of him and what his beating heart felt like whenever I was close enough, which I was at that moment, and so I leaned into those familiar things as if it had been too long since I'd felt them last. Which it wasn't, of course, because hugging wasn't something we did on a regular basis.

We were friends, not lovers. Still it was wonderful to have Max hold me as if I was somehow precious. His blocky body reminded me that no one gets the best of me. Never had and never would as long as he was there to have my back. I lifted my eyes to his and said, "No reporter no matter how good will get an interview out of me."

"Atta girl." He pulled back and disentangled himself from me, after which we found donuts to go with our coffee and spent the better part of an hour rehashing town gossip and not once mentioning lost children or hero dogs or reporters who didn't know enough to leave when the story was finished. By the time he left, the sun was sliding towards evening, and we'd shared a quickie meal of hot dogs and sauerkraut, and there was nothing else to talk about that was happening in town. There's only so much gossip possible in a town the size of Johns Falls.

CHAPTER 11

The next few days I was glad I could work from home because, if I'd left the house, I'd have been snagged before reaching the sidewalk by a middle-aged, thinnish, eagle-eyed reporter who smiled and seemed like a nice person except that she somehow seemed to know what I was doing at every second of every day and at what time I'd likely be leaving the house and available for answering questions. And she had a thousand of them, all having to do with me and my connection to the forest. Instead of dogs, she zeroed in on me.

So I stayed inside more than ever since I'd moved into my nice, rented house. I got a lot of work done. Hollander and Company would love me. I might even get a bonus. But the day finally came when I ran out of food and needed to go shopping or starve to death.

Though, in honesty, I admitted that there was another reason for wanting to be outside. I'm a rural type and, in the time since finding Bobby Deal, spring had come for good, and every rural resident knows that it's imperative to greet each season properly. For spring, that means going outside and feeling the amazing way spring manages to wrap the earth in layers of heat. Hottest is at the tops of the trees where the sun hits hardest, while being still cool and maybe even cold where the earth hides remnants of ice and snow in crannies and behind rocks and beneath logs. It's warm in the layer in between. I walk through that warm middle layer and love it.

The sun-warmed back yard beckoned, as did the sidewalk that would take me to Hollander and Company, with a stop at Jerry's Pizza afterwards, and I decided that I'd let one persistent reporter keep me prisoner in my own house long enough. So I grabbed all the paperwork I'd been polishing ad infinitum for Hollander and Company and sneaked out the back door.

Once in the yard, and after making sure the coast was clear, I slipped out through the side gate in the fence and ran full out across two yards while waving half-heartedly to the neighbors who peered at me from their windows and wondered why I was in such a hurry, until I figured I was far enough away to slow to a walk, at which time I continued at a sedate pace towards the middle of town and people.

I'd missed people during my self-enforced isolation and wondered as I marched along the sidewalk why I'd allowed such a thing to happen and decided I must be more of a coward than I'd realized.

"Hi, Anna, where have you been?" Amos, the blacksmith, who keeps all the expensive horses in the area shod, was curious as he exited his truck and headed for the grain elevator. "Were you sick?" I said that I wasn't and that I'd just been busy and continued on my way, but he'd made me realize that pretending I'd been sick could hide my cowardice if anyone chanced to ask. And they would. Everyone I met would ask what had happened to me because that's the way Johns Falls is. Everyone knows everything about everyone, and they notice when someone goes missing.

"Have you been out of town?" was the next question posed by the next person I met, Carol, who owns a resort so many miles away that she comes to town as seldom as possible and loads her truck till it groans with supplies for her family and everyone in her cabins. "People have been asking about you."

I started to cough. It wasn't hard, I figured I could manage a couple that would sound realistic enough to promote the 'I've been sick' excuse, but then I realized that if I was truly sick I shouldn't be around people and contaminating them, so I stopped my cough almost immediately and stood straight and proud and looked as healthy as possible. "I was a bit under the weather, but just for a while, and I'm fine now." She nodded and returned to loading her pickup while I continued on my way.

"Hey fellow Hollander and Company employee, what's with all that stuff you're carrying?" My co-worker and also-works-at-home friend, Jayce, knew the thick folder of papers in my arms had something to do with work. "Are you trying to put me out of a job or just show me up for the lazy worker I'd like to be?"

I giggled and opened the folder to show Jayce what I'd been doing, and he whistled approval. "Good ideas. Get those shots on a couple of Facebook ads, and we'll all get rich." He reconsidered. "Okay, our bosses will get rich and, since they are nice bosses, we might all get a raise, so keep up the good work."

He handed them back. "Want some help? Anything that'll increase my wages is something I'm willing to do so long as it doesn't interfere with fishing." Jayce fishes every spare second. He'll never marry because he'll never have time to meet any of the lovely ladies I've tried and failed to shove his way. I'm currently looking into women who love fishing as much as he does, but there aren't many people of either sex on the entire earth who fish that much let alone a lot of single women. So he'll probably end up an elderly bachelor.

He matched my steps, though, because he had his own more slender folder to bring to Hollander and Company and, since we were obviously going the same way, we moved together through the warm spring day with just enough tourists strolling the streets to presage the coming vacation season. But for now the streets were empty enough that we didn't have to move aside for anyone.

"Have you met the new woman in town?" He paused long enough to examine a new and very expensive rod and reel in the sporting-goods store without missing a step. "She's sort of a rare bird, but she seems nice."

"New woman?" I shook my head. "I guess I haven't met her."

"Middle-aged or maybe a bit older. Gray hair, anyway, and in good shape physically. Must be some kind of fitness nut."

Something swirled through my mind. His description somewhat resembled the nosy reporter I'd been studiously avoiding. Except for the nice part. But that wasn't possible because surely the middle-aged reporter who'd vaulted over my fence as Max and I ran for the kitchen had given up long ago and left town in search of her next story.

But just in case my nosy reporter was also Jayce's nice, new lady in town, I hurried my steps a bit so as to reach Hollander and Company before any potential reporter saw me and came running. We reached the building with the elegant, red sign proclaiming to the world that it was the home of Hollander and Company without incident and turned over our folders to the receptionist who insisted we stick around long enough for a brief conference with our bosses because they hadn't seen us in so long that they'd been overheard wondering if we still worked there.

When I was called in to my boss' office he smiled. "Been working hard, I see." I nodded, not wishing to dump on him as to just why I'd been working so hard. "You're work is improving. One of these days we'll talk about a raise. Right now, I'd like a list of possible places to run these ads which, by the way, show that you put a lot of time and thought into them." Yep that was what I'd done all right. Put lots of time into them and, since I had nothing else to do with that time – like going outside and enjoying the weather – I'd also put a lot of thought into them.

So, after a few more pleasantries, we parted, with my boss telling me to take it easy for a bit because I'd seriously been working too hard and Hollander and Company didn't have enough work-at-home employees creating wilderness-themed ads to keep up with my recent burst of marketing efforts. I almost ran out of the office. I did run once the door was shut, and then I dropped into a chair, as I indicated that it was Jayce's turn.

When Jayce's conference was also done and he, too, came out smiling, we adjourned to Jerry's for a well-deserved pizza and cappuccinos to celebrate the fact that our bosses had not only remembered we were actual employees, they'd also given us thumbs-up on everything we'd done. "Spring must be good for us," I mentioned as we sashayed out the door and back into the still-warm day. "Boosts our creativity or something."

"We're just eager to get enough stuff done so as to be able to play hooky most of the summer," was his erudite reply as we made our way to the next building and pushed open the door to the heavenly smell of every kind of pizza known to mankind, though the aroma of sausage and pepperoni hung especially heavy in the air. Jerrys is a small-town treasure.

Our procession to a table near the back was a repeat of my walk through town. Everyone wanted to know what had happened to me. Why I'd been out of touch. I didn't know what to say because I didn't like admitting that I'd been hiding from a woman much older, quite a bit thinner, and probably not in as good shape as me. So I once again pulled the I-was-sick-but-I'm-fine-now routine, and everyone bought it, though with a few comments about no particular illness going around at the moment so where had I caught anything?

My neighbor two doors down suggested I'd got in while in the cities.

My neighbor three doors down in the other direction thought I must have caught something in the forest when Max and I were looking for Bobby Deal.

"Uh --- yes, that could be what happened." I spoke vaguely to both at the same time because I didn't want to show favoritism and let everyone think that I could have caught my non-existent cold either place, but someone near the front window – a newcomer in town because he'd lived there only ten years -- thought I meant I'd gotten sick in the forest. "Never heard of trees giving anyone a cold."

Two farmers agreed vigorously. "Being outside should have the opposite effect and increase your immunity instead of giving you a bug."

A bit more information about colds and immunity and the great outdoors was given to the room at large, after which everyone turned back to their own meals and the sound level returned to its usual hum of just above a loud whisper that was characteristic of Jerrys at lunch time.

"Will you want cappuccino?" Jerry asked as he approached our table. He looked at me as if trying to decide if I was still contagious and, after looking me up and down, he evidently decided I was safely over whatever I'd had. "Your mug is still on the shelf in spite of your long absence."

I said cappuccino sounded wonderful -- which it did -- and went to the shelves that lined one wall and was filled with many huge but lovely individual, creatively designed mugs for each of Jerrys' regulars, of whom I am one. I pulled the mug with my name off the shelf along with Jayce's and prepared to return to the table.

And stopped because there was a new mug on the shelf right next to mine. It was exquisite, with gold leaf and a map of the world on it. And a name. "Who's Gwen Wooster?"

A man at the nearest table heard my question. "Gwen? She's that nice lady who's here for a while." He looked around the room. "Anyone know how long she plans on staying?"

There were shrugs saying no one knew exactly, and the speaker continued, "Tall, thin, middle-aged or older, it's hard to say which, and no one knows why she's here precisely, but she seems to like the area, and that shows she has good taste."

"Not a tourist, that's for sure," a woman at the next table said. "Doesn't act like one and doesn't seem interested in the usual tourist things."

A man at the table once removed joined in. "Now that I think about it, she asked about you, Anna. A couple of times. More than a couple."

A shiver went down my spine, and I stared balefully at the lovely gold-leaf mug and wondered what I'd have to do to chase a persistent reporter from town before she had a chance to ingratiate herself further with the locals and keep me prisoner in my own home any longer than she already had.

CHAPTER 12

I stared at the beautiful, tasteful, gold-encrusted mug and spoke without thinking. "This belongs to the reporter who's hounding me."

Everyone stopped what they were doing. The place became as silent as a tomb. Until someone asked cautiously, "Hounding you? How? And why?" Not really believing that someone as nice as Gwen Wooster would hound anyone.

I wished I'd kept my mouth shut, but it was too late. "Because, for some idiot reason, she thinks there's a story about me just because I was with Max when Bobby Deal was found."

The place remained silent as everyone absorbed what I'd said. Then, "You *were* with him, and it's true that no one seemed interested at the time. No reporters anyway."

After a moment, another voice continued, "Which, come to think of it, was wrong. You were there and you helped. You should have been given credit."

A third voice took up that train of thought. "She seems like a nice woman. Maybe she's also a nice reporter and wants to give credit where credit's due because she knows you were wronged."

Before I could snort my derision, a fourth voice joined in. "Or maybe she's a women's libber who decided that you were shoved aside because you're female, and she's out to remedy what she sees as a crime."

Everyone laughed at that, because in Johns Falls women are normally given just as much credit as their men for whatever outdoor work they do, if not more, because they are usually also caring for home and family and everyone knows it. Besides if they aren't given credit, they yell loud and clear until the oversight is remedied.

So why hadn't I yelled when reporters swarmed Max and not me? I'd grown up in Johns Falls and should have done so.

The next voice asked that very question. "You've never been a wimp that I know of." The speaker leaned back in his chair until it balanced on two legs which Jerry watched with a pained expression as one of his chairs strained not to fall apart. "So why didn't you stick yourself into the melee when those reporters were overwhelming Max?"

I took Jayce's and my mugs and made my way slowly back to our table in order to give myself time to think. As I plunked them down in time for Jerry to whisk them away to be filled with his wonderful cappuccinos while knowing without being asked what we each wanted, I turned back to the speaker. "I was glad for not being included in that mess. Glad not to have to answer questions. Glad to not have my life interrupted."

I took a deep breath. "Most of all, I was glad that Max knowing and willingly took the heat, so I didn't have to."

Everyone nodded their heads because, being small town residents or people who lived beyond the town limits in the wilderness on roads that were intentionally too awful for tourists to explore, they understood the value of privacy. And they knew that, even though I lived in town, I often simply walked the couple of blocks to the edge of the forest and then stepped into that vast and awesome place of solitude. And stayed there until my need for privacy was satisfied.

Then an elderly man with a cane and skin so wrinkled that anyone watching would know he'd spent his life out of doors, spoke up. A nice man who didn't think ill of anyone. "She's a nice lady and possibly on the trail of a story. She could be a really good reporter for all we know and sees a story in our Anna. All I know is that she comes in here and talks to everyone as politely as you please and isn't pushy like a lot of people. Especially reporters."

Several heads nodded. Gwendolyn Wooster was well liked, that was clear, and I'd better accept that fact unless I wanted my own personal mug to be removed from Jerrys' wall. I willed myself not to sink through the floor until I realized that about half the people consuming pizza and sipping Jerry's wonderful cappuccinos didn't agree with the elderly man. Instead they sympathized with my desire for privacy. I appreciated that.

"She should leave you alone," one teenaged girl with bright, pink hair said. "Most people want to be invisible and I'd hate it if someone tried to shine a spotlight on me." The elderly man with her who was probably her grandfather because they looked alike except for the hair did his best not to laugh as he inspected her bright head and thought about what she'd said and then choked and spilled half his cappuccino in his lap. He dabbed at it ineffectually with a napkin, while letting me know with zig-zagging eyebrows that he agreed with his daughter about privacy, which made me feel a whole lot better.

Then the door opened, and the brightness of the day shone through the opening, as Max sashayed in floating in the wash of that light and looked around. Saw me. Waggled his head to say he saw me and Jayce and came over. "Having pizza?" I nodded. "Have you guys ordered?"

I shook my head, and he looked at Jayce and said, "I'm hungry too. You want the usual?" Jayce nodded, so Max snagged Jerry, who was on his way to the kitchen. "One extra-large pepperoni and sausage, double the meat, and there's no hurry." Jerry grinned, acknowledging that we were three customers who could gab for hours without realizing it, and he didn't care because he had lots of tables, and it was early spring, so he wasn't busy. Yet.

It didn't take long for our pizza to arrive, and Jayce dived in as if he hadn't eaten for a week. When he finished, he downed the rest of his cappuccino and used a napkin and then hurriedly rose. "I have things to do." He looked at me. "Some of us actually work for a living, and I'd better get home and sit down at my computer and start staring until inspiration comes if I want to fish this summer."

He left, and Max and I stared at the remaining pizza, each taking a slice and pretending to eat while, along with everyone in Jerrys, we tried not to laugh because Jayce hadn't left to leave Max and me alone because he knew there wasn't anything between us because he knows us well. He'd actually gone home to work in order to find more fishing time in the summer.

But because Jayce left so precipitously, there was the slight possibility that perhaps one person in Jerry's might start thinking about our relationship and come with exactly the wrong conclusion because that's how small towns work, and there's always one person who gets things wrong.

We glanced at each other and jointly agreed that the next time we saw Jayce we'd clean his clock for setting us up. He has the weirdest sense of humor and was probably laughing all the way home. Then we just sighed and accepted the inevitable, as we munched on sausage and pepperoni.

Not that anyone gave us any privacy to enjoy our status as imaginary would-be lovers. No way, not in Johns Falls.

A man who'd been watching the whole thing cleared his throat and said, "Anna was snubbed by everyone except that woman reporter. She ought to be rewarded for her part in the rescue, no matter that she thinks being invisible is nice." He nodded shortly. "And that's a fact."

The woman across from him gave a different spin to his remarks. "It wouldn't matter if Anna had been mobbed by reporters. Fame is temporary, so why get all huffy about privacy? She could have taken out a mass murderer, and the fame would last a couple of days, after which she'd go back to being a nobody."

Two tables down a teenager on lunch break from school gobbled a sub sandwich as fast as possible so as to get back to school in time for his next class. "It's all about the dogs, anyway, and not the people who found the kid. The dogs would have kept him alive and safe forever if necessary. I say dogs are wonderful."

There were several 'hear, hears' as he rose and trotted towards the door, watching the clock on the wall as he went. When he was gone, and the door had slammed shut behind him, a couple on lunch break chimed in. "I'd love some publicity. I'd frame the articles and show them to everyone who visits. I'd work it for all it's worth." Then they too rose because the lunch hour was ending, and Jerrys would soon be practically empty. "But everyone is different."

Soon we were almost alone in the now quiet pizza and cappuccino place. We stared at each other and finished our now-cold lunch and then went outside and stood awkwardly for the longest time, just checking out the familiar sights of Johns Falls in the spring. "We should go."

"I have things to do." A lie because my boss had specifically said to take it easy for a while but, for some reason, I felt odd standing beside Max while knowing that if anyone who'd been in Jerry's was watching, they could possibly think we were discussing our love life. "Places to go."

"People to see." Max hunched his shoulders and gave voice to what we were both thinking. "And how dumb are we to concern ourselves with what a few people think?"

His words broke the spell, and I found myself relaxing in spite of the fact that I was beside Max and that lately that had meant being sort of uncomfortable. Unsatisfied. I grinned ruefully. "Why do we care what other people think?" Then I added bravely, "Though, to be honest, I don't actually have anything to do."

He slanted a look towards me. "Me neither. Want to hang out?"

So we went to his house on the edge of the forest and played with his dogs for the entire afternoon and didn't once mention the fact that if past history was any indication, we'd soon be the talk of the town, and how did finding a little lost boy turn us into an item of speculation in the romance department?

CHAPTER 12

As I was getting ready to leave, Max's cell rang. I scooped my own phone from the table and dumped it into my pocket and signaled to him that it was time for me to leave and then headed for the door. I was stopped half-way there by Max's hand on my shoulder. He pulled me back and half-shoved me into a chair and indicated that I should stay until he was finished talking with whomever was on the other end.

Why? Was it important? Probably not, but I sank into a chair and waited until he thumbed off the phone and spoke as the dogs dropped to their haunches and listened because that's what they do. We've never figured out if they understand English, but they certainly seemed to as their ears flicked back and forth.

"We're not done with this rescue thing yet. Bobby Deal is coming to Johns Falls."

"Why?"

"To meet Snow and Frost and give them badges. Seems they are the dogs of the moment, and some dog organization or other has chosen them as the heroes of the month and wants to give them an award and badges."

"They deserve both." The dogs looked from one of

us to the other, huffing their agreement. "So do you. They are your dogs. You raised them from pups."

He snorted. "It's not me. They are the most social dogs in the world. Everyone in Johns Falls raised them, whether they wanted to or not." The dogs' tails thumped agreement as they acknowledged their busy social schedule. "You did too, you know, and Casey taught them everything he knows."

He gave that statement some thought and added to it. "I doubt they'd have found Bobby Deal if Casey hadn't taught them about the forest. Remember how much time your dog spent in the woods with you when he was younger? Hours. Days. Weeks. Years. Well, he taught Snow and Frost everything he knows. I'm sure he showed them every single tree and which side was best to pee on." The dogs' eyes shone with agreement, or because they recognized Casey's name. "I can't count how many times I saw them coming out of the forest with Casey after finishing their jaunts."

He was right, and I knew that it was time for me to go, because I'd been there long enough but I was ridiculously glad when Max said that we should adjourn to his backyard where we could watch the dogs enter and exit the forest on their constant searches that we'd never yet figured out what they were looking for in that green world. "Stick around for a while. I can't believe your boss is holding the whip to you after the amount of work you must have done while hiding from Gwen Wooster."

I wimped out and admitted that my boss had suggested I take it easy and then added that Gwen Wooster was currently the bane of my existence.

As we grabbed pop from his refrigerator and

dropped into lounge chairs behind his house, Max continued our conversation as if we'd not stopped talking, a not-unusual thing because we'd always found things to talk about, something our teachers had often commented on before sending us to the principal's office for being inattentive in class.

In Max's tree-dotted back yard, I found myself relaxing all the way to my toes, and it was about time. The forest does that to me. It sends something through my body that calms me no matter what's going on in my life, and it worked this time too, even though Gwen Wooster had truly gotten to me more than anyone else ever had. The forest that was so close and the breeze on my face took away her strange ability to tie me into a knot, and I lay back in the lounge chair and let the remainder of Max's words flow over and around me, as I peered at him from half-closed eyes and was glad that we'd been friends forever.

I felt as if I was existing on some other plane -- some better place -- as I watched the light come and go with the motion of leaves that were skittering aimlessly in the breeze and changing the dappled shade of Max's backyard from daytime to evening and back again in the blink of an eye as the sun waned. And I wondered, as I'd been wondering a lot lately while watching Max relaxing so close to me, what had changed about him and why it had happened and why I couldn't seem to quantify that change. All I knew was that something was different.

Then I grew attentive because he was talking about Gwen Wooster, and I'd better listen because he might have something helpful to say. Some suggestion as to how to avoid her.

"What say I call the people in charge of the ceremony giving medals to the dogs and ask that you be included?"

"Are you refusing to take the heat any longer?" I wouldn't blame him.

"I'm suggesting a way for you to show that reporter how you were involved with Bobby Deal's rescue."

"Explain, please."

"If she sees that you were there all along and that the reason you were ignored is because other reporters forgot about you in their eagerness to focus on the dogs, then she might stop pestering you."

"It might work. What do you think?"

"I think it's worth a try." He waved the dogs off and sent them tumbling into the yard instead of his lap, and they obligated by racing each other to the nearest trees. "I can call the event organizers right now."

I thought still more. "It might work, and then I'll be free of her forever. If it doesn't work – "

"What else can she think?"

So he made the call, and it was arranged that I'd be with him and the Malamutes when Bobby Deal gave them medals. The presenters were happy to have me. They'd wondered what was going on with my absence because they'd seen me when Max and I emerged from the forest when Bobby was found, but they'd politely kept their distance in case there was a reason for my hanging back.

So we toasted our plan with a clink of pop cans and spent the next couple of hours watching Snow and Frost wandering in and out of the forest as it grew darker and still darker while wondering how they'd react to having medals hung around their necks by a little boy with cameras everywhere. Because, according to the presenters, it was going to be a big deal. A very big deal. Possibly a world-wide phenomenon.

When the day turned cool, as spring days do, and the sun finally fell completely behind the trees, and the dogs were still exploring to the point of no light anywhere, we still sat in those chairs and sipped pop, though much slower than earlier and still talked now and then about nothing in particular though, as with the pop, the talk slowed to a trickle of nothing important.

And we watched the evening turn into night. Max considered the few remaining faint pink streaks on the western horizon that were visible through the few empty splotches between the trees, and he turned to me and grinned lazily. "It's what we do for entertainment in Johns Falls. Watch evening come and spread across everything until it becomes night."

"A fabulous show, and it's free."

And still we sat and gazed at the deepening dark until it became the color of black velvet and petted the dogs as they slowed down and settled between us while wagging their tails and laying their heads on their paws as they considered us with wisdom in those huge eyes.

Unexpectedly, Max rose and came to me. Took my empty pop can and tossed it into a garbage can along with his. Dropped low enough to sit on the edge of my chair as I moved to make room for his bulky body. Said nothing, but stared at me as if he'd never seen me before and, somehow, I thought that might actually be what was happening because I was definitely seeing him in a new light lately, so possibly he'd be doing the same with me.

Then he leaned close and kissed me. A slow,

lingering kiss that could mean everything or nothing. And then, without speaking, he rose and got us each another can of pop from the house, though he was followed by the dogs who informed him that they'd been patient enough as we sat outside but that dinner was overdue, and could he feed them please?

I called after him. "No more pop. Something warm like coffee. Or tea."

So it was a while before he returned, and by that time whatever had happened between us was over and done with. But not forgotten because, as time passed and the night grew still darker and night birds came out and night sounds reached out to us from the forest in their subtle and strange way, I was glad for the dark because it saved me from having to talk about what had – or had not – happened.

And when he repeated that kiss as I left for home, I didn't know how to act, and I suspected neither did he. But I didn't push him away. Didn't pull him closer either.

And as I covered the brief distance between our houses, covering those few blocks that was most of Johns Falls, I wondered what had just happened even as I hugged new and unexpected feelings close and found myself stepping quicker than usual through the town I'd known forever while wondering how I'd not noticed before what a truly lovely town it was.

CHAPTER 13

The ceremony honoring Snow and Frost took place two weeks following the phone call. It evidently took that long to arrange things, though I couldn't see why, because it was held outside in the park where the helicopter had landed and made Bobby and the dogs famous, and it was free to anyone who wanted to come which was just about everyone in town plus everyone who'd been involved in the rescue so it was a good thing the park was spacious. The grassy field was crowded enough that the fragile spring grass was in danger of being trampled to death and tents were once more erected with food and drinks for everyone, and there was a tiny raised platform for the dogs and important people. Which included me.

I looked around for Max and security, while hating to admit that when large groups of people were involved, I want someone between them and me. Like Max. I spotted him emerging from the food tent with two Styrofoam cups of coffee, two donuts, and two dogs chasing around him in circles.

He was looking around. I waved, and he spotted me and waved back carefully so as not to spill coffee, and joined me, followed by Snow and Frost, who began circling around me and pushing until Max and I were practically in each other's laps. He handed me one of each of his carefully held provisions and led me to the platform.

"Do we have designated seats?" Hopefully mine would be in the back.

"Probably, but I don't know which is which, so I'm opting for the front and maximum exposure." He grinned wolfishly as he stuffed the remainder of his donut in his mouth and swallowed, then rinsed with the last of his coffee, and then sighed and continued, "Because this is a once in a lifetime thing for me, so I'm going for all the adulation I can get. For the dogs of course, and not because I like attention." Which he loved as much as the dogs did. The dogs and Max were alike in many ways.

"I'll sit behind everyone." Hide was more like it, and he knew what I was thinking as he shook his head slowly at my well-known dislike of publicity, but he didn't pull me into the chair next to him. Instead he simply dropped into the chair beside the one in the center of the platform that obviously belonged to whomever was in charge of this whole medal thing. The dogs settled in front of him and gazed out over the throngs of people with their tails thumping against the wood platform eyes while taking in everything and enjoying the day. They were social dogs.

I claimed the chair behind Max and was grateful for his large, blocky frame that hid me from everyone and hid everyone from me, until he said over his shoulder in sotto voice. "I hope you are visible to that reporter who's making your life miserable because that's why you're here. To let her see that you aren't being ignored so she'll decide you are part of the story after all and will leave you alone."

He waited for me to change chairs, which I did, sliding obdurately into the one next to him that left me visible to every single gawking person in the field, and I was sure they were all gawking at me. "That's better." He didn't laugh, for which I was grateful.

I soon learned that I was wrong about the chair in the middle of the platform. It wasn't for whomever was in charge. It was for Bobby Deal himself, which I learned when a car pulled up that was instantly surrounded by reporters and other media types. First Bobby's parents got out and then Bobby himself. He looked around and spotted the dogs and Max and me. A smile burst across his face that rivaled the sun, and he broke through those media types as if they didn't exist and made a beeline for Snow and Frost.

In seconds he was on the stage and hugging the Malamutes who responded by licking his face and generally slobbering all over him. Then his parents arrived and several other people who seemed to be in charge of the ceremonies, and everyone found seats, and one elderly man with a fringe of gray hair tested the microphone and then gestured for the crowd to quiet down.

It did eventually, after the man thumped on the mic several times to make it send out horrible squawks, and then everyone listened while practically everyone on the platform said something or other about dogs in general and Snow and Frost in particular. Then Bobby Deal slipped two huge gold medals on purple ribbons over the dogs' heads as people jostled for the best view and cameras went off and everyone clapped and stomped and whistled and Snow and Frost stood there like royalty and accepted all the adulation as if it was their due. Which it was.

Then the official part of the ceremony was over. The gray-haired man said there was free cake and drinks for everyone in the food tent and bones for the dogs, so if they meandered in that direction everyone, both human and canine, would get what they liked. The stampede that followed was slow and orderly but unmistakably eager.

Max and I were left alone on the platform with the dogs and Bobby Deal and the reporters who wanted news more than free food and who'd clambered up to take the places of the important people. Bobby's parents had joined those looking for cake and drinks, after making sure Max and I would look after their son, who clearly wanted to stay with his beloved dogs for as long as possible.

The reporters spread across the platform with a few stooping to hug Snow and Frost as they passed because they were obviously dog people, while the rest closed in on Max and me. All had cameras of one kind or another and were taking pictures non-stop including the bane of my life, Gwen Wooster, who ignored the dogs completely in favor of me and who managed to slide through the throng until she was so close that a piece of paper wouldn't fit between us.

She smiled and opened her mouth to ask questions, then snapped it shut again when Bobby began speaking after backing up to me in defense against the sudden onslaught of people. He fit himself into my arms much as he'd done in the forest beside the tiny stream where he'd been found.

"You gave me water." He snuggled deeper against me, and I wrapped my arms around him protectively This might not be the forest, but reporters posed an equally scary kind of danger.

He was clean and warm and smelled like little boys should. "You gave me a sandwich." I nodded and every reporter moved closer and listened and held out microphones while clicking cameras and making notes. Gwen Wooster listened so hard that she held her breath. "Then you told that man to climb a tree."

I nodded and cameras clicked. "He did climb a tree, and then he called someone, and a helicopter came and brought you home."

Bobby burrowed deeper into my body as he sighed and remembered. "The man said you found me." A sub-vocal sound swept through the reporters as they realized this as was aspect of the rescue that they'd missed. "Because you knew how. You knew where I was."

You could have heard a pin drop as they digested this new information and moved closer. How to deflect their well-honed reportorial instincts? "I spend a lot of time in the forest." What else to say? How to make them think finding Bobby had been almost accidental? I didn't know so I went silent.

"Do you like trees?" Bobby gazed into my eyes.

"I suppose so." It might work. "Yes, I like trees a lot. As you like butterflies."

He grinned. "I do like butterflies." His face went dark as he recalled that day. "I followed one, and I got lost."

I hugged him until the darkness disappeared. "That's how I found you. Because you like butterflies, and I like trees, so I looked for trees with lots of butterflies under them. And there you were."

His grin grew. "Will you take me there? To see more butterflies?" Then he remembered what had happened when he followed butterflies before and darkness threatened to return until he cast a look towards Snow and Frost. "Please bring the dogs. I want the dogs to come too."

I hugged him harder. "Someday, maybe. Right now, though, I think your parents are looking for you."

He sighed a mighty sigh. "I suppose so." Looked at me with all the wisdom of a toddler. "They don't let me go anywhere alone. Not any more."

The reporters laughed, we all did, and then the group slowly dissolved, with Bobby's parents grabbing him and heading for a bench with cake and Kool-Aid for him, and the reporters followed after glancing from the dogs to Bobby in an agony of indecision. They went with Bobby because he was more likely to give them a story than Snow and Frost.

All the reporters except Gwen Wooster. She looked at me shrewdly. "So you like trees." An innocent statement that wasn't innocent at all. Her eyes lit with reportorial zeal.

I kept things casual. Tried to anyway. "I was born and raised in the North Woods. Everyone around here likes trees." Max nodded agreement while, in a way that seemed accidental and wasn't, he wrapped an arm around my shoulders and turned me slightly away so she had to go through him to get to me. My childhood friend protecting me once again from a schoolyard bully.

"I suspect there's more to it than that."

I wasn't a child any more. I shouldn't need

protecting. So I moved. Peered around Max and gave her what I hoped was a baleful stare. "That's all there was. I looked for the right trees." Clearly a lie.

Which she recognized. Her eyes grew even brighter as my words solidified her belief that something special and unusual and possibly occult was going on.

I felt Max sigh because I'd done it now. Ruined all his hard work convincing her that nothing was going on. Oh dear. What now?

I backtracked. "What I mean is that there's nothing special about me finding Bobby."

She smiled. I've seen snakes smile nicer. "Everyone's special in some way or another."

I gulped. "Not me. I'm just your average, normal, everyday person."

"Who likes trees and knows where to find boys lost in the forest."

"It was luck."

"Then you're luckier than most people." She leaned closer and around Max's body until we were face to face. "And that luck is a story as soon as you're willing to be interviewed." She waved a hand a few times. "People are fascinated with stories of lucky people. Like lottery winners." She got so close that we were almost nose to nose. "In a way you won the lottery, but it wasn't money you found, it was a little lost boy." She pulled back, possibly because Max's face turned thundercloud dark. "Everyone would love to hear about your lucky trip through the forest."

I opened my mouth to agree to an interview because she was being way more persistent than I'd have thought possible and perhaps that was the best way to get rid of her, but before I could make a sound Max, face even darker and more thundercloud-like, moved me subtly away from Gwen Wooster and stuck his face in hers.

I give her credit because she knew when to quit. She took one look at Max and shut up and then slowly, ever so slowly, she backed away until she almost fell off the platform. Grabbing a nearby post to regain her balance, she then continued away from me, though more from Max, actually, and his fierce and eminently threatening demeanor.

When she was gone and I was held so close that I could feel Max through the cloth of his shirt, I felt his body shudder. Shake. And then when Gwen Wooster was out of sight and he couldn't hold it any longer, he put his head back and laughed.

"She bought it." He laughed harder and let go of me because he couldn't hold me and laugh at the same time. "She actually believed I was going to do something nasty if she harassed you any longer." Tears of laughter ran down his cheeks. "I should go to Hollywood. I'm that good."

I pushed his chest with a finger. "You're not that good, but I'm glad it worked." I returned to my place against his chest, and we sat there for the longest time with one of his arms casually around me and our legs all over the place as a late afternoon breeze rose ad ruffled our hair and tangled it together. Mine was longer, of course, so he had to brush it away in order to see, but that was a minor movement that didn't interfere with our contemplation of life in general and female reporters in particular.

We watched as people started leaving. Cars exited the field until there were only a few here and there, and crews came to dismantle everything including the platform we were on.

I didn't want to leave. I wanted Max's arms to stay around me all warm and comfortable and known. But as several men approached, Max sighed and removed his arms and untangled us from each other. "Time to go home, and I think it worked."

"I'm afraid all it did was make that reporter more determined than ever to get a story out of me."

He kind of sagged. "Perhaps. If so, then we're back to the first plan. Avoid her at all costs, and I'll help in any way possible."

"I'd move in with you except if I disappeared then your place would be the first place she'd look."

"You're right about that. But we'll think of something."

And so we left it at that as we jumped from the platform so the workers could take it apart and throw the lumber in the back of a truck and be done with the day's celebration.

CHAPTER 14

During the next few days, as I looked ahead to the next round of at-home work on behalf of Hollander and Company and tried to make it up to Casey for not taking him to Snow and Frost's celebration, I thought a lot about my run-in with Gwen Wooster. Specifically how to get rid of her since showing up at the celebration hadn't worked.

To think more clearly, I took a careful walk through town without running into her and then beyond, to Max's place, except he wasn't home so, instead of conferring with him, I ended up sitting in his yard staring at the forest mere yards away while waiting for an epiphany because surely I deserved some good luck. Some kind of psychic insight, but the forest I'd once thought I had a psychic connection with just sat there being a forest. Of course I got no psychic vibes but it could be because I'm as psychic as a block of wood.

As my mind kind of detoured through my life and all kinds of odd memories surfaced, I realized that every time I'd been down in the dumps or needed a new direction in life, I'd gone for a walk in the very forest I was staring at now, and each time I'd come out feeling better.

Somehow, in the depths of the north woods, beneath the shelter of those evergreens and birches, I'd always found peace, and right now peace waited for me there, and all I had to do was cross the yard and enter the forest. I knew as surely as I knew my own name that the peace I'd find in the forest would be as good as an actual solution to the problem of Gwen Wooster. I decided to take that walk.

But first things first. I turned away from the trees and headed home because it was too late to do anything that day, but I determined that the next morning would find me in the forest with a pack that would include a substantial lunch, mosquito repellant, and whatever else I could think of to keep me comfortable and in good health, so I wouldn't have to emerge until I'd figured out what to do about the reporter who was now the bane of my life. If it took all day, so be it.

Besides peace, though, it was spring and the winter had been long and hard and the snow too deep to go anywhere, so it was about time I got out of the house and once more visited my favorite place in the whole world. Got my fix of forest.

So sunrise the next day found me filling Casey's food and water dishes which made him thump his tail dejectedly because he knew it meant he'd be alone, and then I peered carefully everywhere I could see to make sure Gwen Wooster wasn't around. Then I pulled on my backpack and quietly slipped out the back door and headed through a town that was slowly coming awake.

I avoided Max's place because I wanted to be alone and knew that he'd offer to come with me. Maybe insist because, though he believed in my ability to find my way in the forest, he worried about other things. Broken legs, he'd say, or getting tangled in thorns, or running into a pack of wolves, or a bear or two, or a cougar. Anything could happen, he'd remind me with a glowering expression and a reminder that Casey was now too old to go with me, and that it's never a good idea to go into the forest alone.

But today I decided foolishly that peace was more important than safety, so I avoided his place by a good city block and by choosing instead to walk farther down to the waterfall that gave Johns Falls its name. I crossed the river on the plank bridge the town had built to better admire the water splashing on the rocks below. And stepped into the forest. And disappeared.

Once beneath the trees, I took a deep, cleansing breath and remembered why I'd gone on that walk all those years ago as a little girl. Because something about the forest made me feel good. Right. Happy. In tune with nature and with God. I kept walking, but slowed to almost a stop in order to better examine everything.

The snow had been deep that winter and hadn't been gone all that long, so I expected the forest to still hold bits and pieces of the white stuff in hidden places, but no snow appeared even though I looked, because it could stay until June, but I decided that the unusually warm days when Bobby Deal's family had gone camping had finished off winter. Frankly I didn't miss it.

The wildflowers were abundant. Nothing large and showy that I could find beyond the bright yellow swamp lilies, but here and there were touches of color so slight as to be almost lost among the brown of left-over winter and the green of a spring already looking towards summer.

Then I spied what Bobby Deal had seen. A butterfly. Possibly the same one he'd followed because, when I thought about it, I was close to the place where he'd entered the forest. I watched, fascinated, and lost in thoughts of the little boy who'd caused such a commotion because he liked butterflies.

I leaned against a tree trunk and watched the butterfly until it disappeared. Soon after, as I'd expected, another appeared and flew about for a while. Then it too disappeared in the same general direction as the first.

They were repeating the flight pattern that Max and I had followed that had eventually led us to Bobby. But when I thought about it, when we'd found him by that creek, there hadn't been many butterflies in the area. Hardly any. Why not?

I don't know how long I stood and watched butterflies coming and going and, as I watched, I became absolutely certain that Bobby hadn't found the butterfly haven he'd been looking for and neither had we. Because, though there were just a few flying around at a time, taken all together there were a lot of butterflies flitting through that forest. A whole lot.

So where did they come from? More importantly, where were they going?

I decided to find out. I'd follow them carefully, and this time I'd be thinking about butterflies instead of a little lost boy. It would be something to do with my day in the forest, a purpose, a goal for my wandering feet and a celebration of beauty because butterflies are gorgeous.

If I found that butterfly haven, maybe I'd call Bobby or email him to let him know about the place where all the butterflies congregated. He'd like that. I'd take pictures with my cell phone. It might not work for making calls, but I was pretty sure the camera worked, and Bobby would like pictures.

It was slow going. Several times I stopped following the butterflies and dropped to the ground to take a break because the farther into the forest I went the more difficult the terrain became. Soon I was in an area that even I, the woman who knew the forest better than anyone else in the area, wasn't familiar with. A strange place. A place I suspected no one had been for perhaps hundreds of years or more, and the reason was clear. The undergrowth grew so thick that no sane person would venture there.

Which meant I was insane as I examined the tangled undergrowth ahead of me and once more set off to follow those butterflies and find where they were going. I took one cautious step after another, while pulling tangled underbrush aside after examining each branch and after pulling on the gloves that I'd thankfully brought, because most of those bushes had thorns that would rip my skin to shreds if I so much as touched them in the wrong way. But though my progress was slow, I did move ahead along the same path as the butterflies.

The butterflies, of course, flitted through the thorn bushes with ease. Once, I heard a sound behind me of some rather large animal tramping through the forest, but I wasn't concerned because nothing larger than a rabbit would attempt to penetrate the thicket I was proceeding through so carefully. So I blocked the sound from my mind and continued on.

I saw why the thorn bushes grew so abundantly.

There'd been a blow-down a long time ago. Almost every tree had gone over and now lay on the ground with their trunks covered by moss and half-way through the process of decaying. The bushes had grown quickly where the trees had fallen, outpacing the new, young trees that were just now beginning to resemble trees that would eventually take over and kill the bushes. But, for now, the bushes reigned supreme, and the sun shone down hot and lush on them and all their thorns in this one tiny spot in the forest.

Moving so slowly and untangling bushes and pushing them carefully aside so as not to be torn to shreds, I wasn't able to look ahead more than the next step. I stopped every so often to wait for a butterfly so as to keep on track and eventually find the place they must be headed towards.

So it was a complete surprise when I took another step that I expected would be blocked by still more thorn bushes and found empty space instead. Wondering what was ahead, I stepped cautiously into the cleared area and looked around.

And gasped in awe.

In the small clearing from the downed trees and darting among the bushes that were taking advantage of the blow-down to grow like weeds, were dozens of butterflies flying near and beneath the single tree in the absolute center of the spot. Dozens? Not dozens, hundreds, maybe thousands, both large and small and all fluttering in the sunlight and gleaming and moving in a symphony of color and beauty that no one knew existed because no one had penetrated the thorn-covered thicket to reach this special place. Until now. Until me.

As I stared open-mouthed, I heard again the sound
of that animal moving still closer but I felt no fear
because no animal with any sense – or the ability to feel
the prick of thorns – would follow me here. And, sure
enough, as I listened, the sound diminished and
whatever it was backed off and presumably went
elsewhere, leaving me to continue admiring the display
before me.

I was awed by the colors, the silent beauty, and the
motion of the butterflies flying in unison in a roiling
cloud that wound around and over the bushes before
rising steeply to the sun only to drop just as
precipitously and repeat the process all over again.
Only this cloud had physical form, and color, and life.

I'd never seen anything like it in my entire life and
could have stood there forever taking it all in. But
knowing time was passing and that soon the sun would
be hidden by the surrounding forest, I pulled my cell
phone from my pocket and began snapping pictures for
Bobby Deal.

But that animal behind me, against all common
sense, hadn't gone away after all, because I could hear
its movement coming closer taking slow, cautious steps
that followed the same path I'd made through the
thicket. It was using the trail I'd cleared to come here,
and it didn't have to worry about getting pricked
because I'd made a trail for it almost as nice as if it
were walking along a path in a park. Darn.

I looked about. Saw a place on the other side of the
thicket that was beside a tree with branches I could
climb if the animal proved dangerous, so I went through
the bushes carefully so as to leave no obvious trail for it
to follow and slipped behind that tree, where I became

as silent as possible and peered out carefully to see what kind of animal I'd have to contend with while remembering Max's many admonitions over numerous years about not going into the forest alone because dangerous animals roamed there freely.

And stifled a gasp as Gwen Wooster stepped into the clearing.

CHAPTER 15

She must have followed me. Unless she knew the forest as well as I do and knew where I was headed, which wasn't likely given that she'd spent her life elsewhere.

Which meant that she could get lost going back if I disappeared and she didn't have me to follow. Darn. I debated the ethics of leaving her to her fate. Did I care? I selfishly decided that if I hadn't heard her loud and clear as she followed me through my favorite woods, she must have been far enough behind me that she couldn't have followed me, she'd only followed my trail and, if she could do that, then she could follow it in reverse and get back home all by herself.

Convoluted logic, but it worked for me. Besides, if she got lost, she deserved whatever happened. I thought hard and managed to see that train of thought as a truth that meant I didn't have to worry about Gwen Wooster, and I fought my guilty feelings to a standstill.

As I studied her, I realized that she was as awestruck by the beauty of the butterfly haven as I'd been, which actually made me almost like her a little. A bit. Her mouth hung open, and she turned around and around and around to better take in the glory of the living picture she'd inadvertently stepped into. Her camera started clicking and continued nonstop as she captured the uniqueness of the place even better than I'd done with my cell phone.

She was so busy admiring the butterflies that she wouldn't have heard me if I'd have been an elephant crashing through the underbrush. Possibly she'd forgotten I existed. She was a reporter, after all, and the butterfly oasis would make a beautiful story. She'd be famous.

So I could leave. I wanted to back off a bit, turn around, and be on my way, only first I had to figure out how to push through the tangle of thorn bushes without announcing my presence, which could mean I'd have to choose between making noise avoiding thorns or bleed to death. I decided that whatever happened to me in the process of leaving the butterfly oasis was better than watching her zone out on butterflies because, eventually, she'd grow bored and start looking for me and, given time, the sun would pass overhead enough that the brilliant light would turn to shadow, and this amazing place would once again be just another slice of forest that happened to hold a lot of insects. When that happened, she'd end her butterfly quest and discover me hiding behind a tree.

I had to leave quickly. I took one cautious step backwards. Felt thorns penetrate my sleeves and my pants, my back being protected by the pack-back. I stopped because going on was impossible and wondered what to do next.

And felt arms wrapping around me, a face coming as close to mine as the back-pack allowed and heard a whispered voice. Max's voice. "Shhhhh. I'll get us out of here without Ms. Wooster suspecting a thing." Then, even lower, "There's a path with fewer thorns just a few yards away." And a third time, "I'll get you there. Trust me."

Trust Max? I'd trust him with my life.

I very, very slowly turned until we were face to face, after which Max nodded shortly to remind me to stay silent, turned around himself and, one baby step at a time, led me through the thorns along a path that he'd cleared much as the one I'd cleared for myself that Gwen Wooster had followed. And we slowly, quietly, and with no more than a half dozen pricks, made our way out of the thorn thicket and into the larger, quieter woods where huge evergreens prevented thick undergrowth beneath their many limbs.

We walked out of that area as easily as strolling through a park, and the ground was so thickly carpeted with pine needles that any sound we might make was instantly muffled into nothingness. But we didn't talk because we didn't want to take chances. Gwen Wooster had been savvy enough to follow me through the forest, she might be good enough to hear a conversation even through the sound barrier of those pines.

Where had her peripatetic life taken her that she'd learned how to make her way through uncharted areas? What adventures had she had? What wildernesses had she traversed? Never mind, she was the enemy, and all I wanted was as far away from her as possible.

When we happened upon an area of younger pines with less dense shade, a spot where dappled sun managed to filter through the branches bringing with it the promise of future summer warmth while also being far enough from the butterfly oasis that there was no chance of the reporter hearing us, we dropped to the ground, leaned against a fallen log, pulled out the substantial lunch I'd packed, and sighed in relief and total, pure enjoyment.

"I saw you go into the forest." Max answered the question I hadn't asked.

"I stayed away from your place. Intentionally." No use pretending I hadn't been avoiding him. He knew better, because he knew me.

"I wasn't home. The dogs wanted to go for a walk, so we went along the river, which is one of their favorite places to meander."

Which was where I'd entered the forest. "And you saw me."

"Yep." He didn't even try to hide the sanctimonious timbre in his voice. Nor the laughter. Nor the superiority. He just slanted a look at me from eyes that were so dark and deep that I could swim in them. But he didn't say what he was thinking and didn't laugh, and I loved him for that.

Loved him? Yes, as a friend because friends can love each other in a friend kind of way, can't they? Sort of.

But the word 'love' sent thoughts of other kinds of love flitting momentarily through my mind until, in disgust, I pushed all thoughts of romantic love to the back of my mind and chomped down on a ham and cheese sandwich because, since I'd left without breakfast, I was starved. Max must be also because he turned away from me and was doing the same, sighing in contentment when he finished the first sandwich and reached for another. Good thing I'd packed enough food for a week. I suspected that when we finally left our impromptu picnic area, albeit one sans tables and benches, there'd be nothing left but a few crumbs.

Our hands met now and then digging out another sandwich, can of pop, or handful of cookies, and each time I remembered that odd thought about romantic love because, though I'd tried, I hadn't managed to push it completely away. In fact, as I sat there beside Max while taking in his scent that was a mix of evergreens and after-shave, I wondered how many kinds of love exist. Because sure as the sun comes up in the morning, I felt at least one kind right then, and the recipient of that feeling was Max.

Not the all-consuming kind of love, of course. Not the romantic kind. But some kind. And the notion grew in me until I said, "I love you, Max."

He choked. Spit out a mouthful of sandwich. Looked at me, wide-eyed, until I laughed, after which he relaxed somewhat while still staring at me from the corner of his eyes because he didn't dare look at me straight on until I managed to stop laughing enough to explain. "Don't worry, not that kind of love. I'm not going to pounce on you. But you're a true friend and that's love, isn't it?"

He thought that over. Tilted his head as if doing so would make his thought process clearer. Inspected the ground in front of us, the insects inches from his brown, leather boots, the tiny, blue wildflowers that grew in defiance of the shadow world beneath the trees. And said, "Yes it is. I think."

Then he grabbed another sandwich and ate it with gusto. I wasn't sure whether he was full or merely needed something between us. A barrier. Something that would allow him to not say any more.

Did he need a barrier? Wasn't our friendship solid enough for us say whatever came into our minds? Or not. I decided the smartest thing I could do was change the subject. "Do you think Gwen Wooster will be alright by herself?" I added, "Not that I care."

He harrumped. "She'd better be woods-wise. That butterfly place is pretty remote."

That wasn't what I wanted to hear. I wanted him to say that of course she could take care of herself. "She followed me. She was woods-wise enough that I didn't know she was there for the longest time and, when I heard her, I thought she was an animal."

"I'll bet she's followed dozens of people. Hundreds. And they all ran as fast as you did whenever she got close." He leaned back and examined what he could see of the sky through all that green stuff. "So I'm guessing she's ended up in some strange places and is pretty good at finding her way back."

I nodded agreement, relieved that we thought alike, and we gathered our left-overs and rose, stuffing them into the back-pack preparatory to returning to civilization. We examined our trail and decided it wasn't noticeable enough for anyone to follow, the pine needles having sprung back after we passed. Not even Gwen Wooster would know we'd been there. "We can leave now with a good conscience. We can go home."

CHAPTER 16

We headed along the divide between the old-growth trees and the younger ones, knowing that line was where logging had stopped many years ago and that following it was like following a road that would lead to the river and, at the end of the line of trees, the park beside the waterfall.

We started out at a brisk pace. Then we slowed. Looked at each other and then away. Slowed still more. Then, finally, we stopped. Our shoulders slumped as we acknowledged what we'd been carefully avoiding.

"We should go back."

I nodded miserably. "We should make sure she's okay."

"Because she's a human being."

"We'd rescue her if she was lost just like we did Bobby Deal."

We both sighed. "So we return to the butterfly oasis."

I leaned against an evergreen, wishing I had the courage to do what I'd threatened, to leave Ms. Wooster to her fate whatever that would be. But I didn't, so I nodded slowly. "We go back to the butterflies."

Max tried to put a good face on our decision. "I like butterflies."

I also tried to be semi-happy with our decision. "We'll see lots of them, and they are beautiful."

He didn't want to go back any more than I did. "Their beauty will be worth the trip."

We made up reasons to go back that had nothing to do with feeling guilty. "Making sure Gwen Wooster is safe is incidental. The butterflies are what are important."

He nodded so hard that his hair flew every which way. "We can hide behind that tree you hid behind. She won't know we're there."

"And we'll make sure she's safe while we're watching the butterflies."

We both knew the real reason for returning. "We'll follow her home."

We both thought about that a bit, not liking the idea but accepting that it was the prudent course of action because if we didn't, she might get lost, and we'd have to find her. "Someday when we have time, we'll come back to see the butterflies."

"They could be gone by then. Butterflies are temporary."

"We'll go soon. Tomorrow, maybe."

So we agreed and slowly made our way back along the path to the butterfly thicket. The closer we got, the quieter we moved, and the slower. "We don't want her to hear us." A whisper.

"We don't want her to know we're there." Another whisper, even lower.

Slower still we went, one step at a time, while avoiding twigs that could give us away, and keeping large trees between us and the trail ahead. It took the better part of an hour to cover the ground we'd done in much less time earlier. But eventually we neared the butterfly oasis in the exact spot where I'd hidden behind a tree and Max had showed up. Once we were behind it, we peered carefully around its trunk.

"She's still here." Max's whisper was full of surprise. "And she's still taking pictures."

My answering whisper was equally surprised. How long before a reporter would normally grow tired of butterflies? "They'll make a wonderful story."

He snorted in derision, and Gwen Wooster heard and looked our way. Max clapped his hand over his mouth, and we waited with bated breath but, seeing nothing even though she stared hard, she eventually returned to snapping pictures. And to following the butterflies as they moved from bush to bush, holding out her hands and standing as still as a statue until one or more would light on them. Smiling a private smile of delight that made me almost like her. Almost.

We settled in for a long wait because we were determined to follow at a discrete distance when she left in order to make sure she was okay without being observed, which meant we waited for almost an hour, during which time she scoured the tiny clearing, snapping pictures not only of butterflies but also of every bit of flora and fauna in the place. Tiny purple flowers. Towering birches, forced to grow as tall as the nearby evergreens in order to reach the sun and, of course, the ever-present thorn bushes that she stayed as far away from as we did. Those she snapped with a shudder that I well understood and sympathized with. Her shirt was made of tough fabric but there were rents in it.

Eventually the sun passed beyond the cleared area, and shadows quickly swept across the tiny space. With a sigh of regret and one last smile at three butterflies that landed on her still form, a smile of true happiness that I was sure she'd never allow if she knew she was being watched, she replaced the lens cap on what I was sure was an expensive camera and packed it into the case she wore on her shoulder.

Max leaned close to my ear. "She likes butterflies."

"And interfering in people's lives."

He pressed his mouth into my shoulder to keep his laughter from being heard. Stayed that way a long time because Gwen Wooster, when she relaxed, was very funny indeed. Raised his head and wiped tears of laughter from his cheeks. Started to whisper something else and thought better of it. Probably didn't want to laugh any more and suffocate in my shirt.

But he had a point. Gwen Wooster clearly loved the tiny clearing and the even tinier lives that fluttered past as they went about their business. What plants did butterflies prefer? I didn't know and determined to find out when we returned to civilization and the internet. Maybe I'd plant something to attract them.

Glancing at Max, I knew he was thinking the same thing, and he dared another whisper so low as to almost be unheard. "Bobby Deal has good taste in insects." I nodded and he buried his face in my shoulder again to avoid sneezing from my hair tickling his nostrils. Then he sensibly backed away enough that cool air rushed in between us and I unexpectedly found myself reaching deep into my thoughts to see how I felt about that slight separation, that coolness, because, oddly enough, I did feel something, and I didn't recall that happening before during all the years I'd known him, all the times we'd gotten into trouble together, all the times we'd done things as a team.

I missed his closeness. The coolness bothered me, the light seemed slightly dimmer, though that could be just the passing of the sun beyond view.

Then Gwen Wooster moved. Sighed. Looked around one last time and, after regarding the thorn bushes with a grimace, stepped out into the thicket and towards home in a ground-eating pace that would get her there in short order.

We followed, not going through the butterfly oasis because it was too open and she might see us. We went a lot slower than she did, being very careful not to make any sound or get close enough for her to see us if she happened to glance back, so it took a while to circle both the oasis and the thorn thicket and find her path and then track her through the woods. But we told ourselves that was good because it meant we were far enough behind that she'd not likely notice us.

It never occurred to either of us that she might not continue that ground-eating stride. That she might slow down and take time to see the forest, or to rest now and then, or to double-check where she was going. We should have known she'd check her whereabouts since she was in unfamiliar territory. Of course she would.

But we never thought those things, and we didn't realize that we were catching up with her until we heard a shout from not far ahead. "Who's there?"

We froze. Backed until we found a huge tree to hide behind. Stood as still as statues and waited to be discovered. Looked at each other and wondered how we'd managed to be so dumb.

We held our breaths as long as possible and then breathed slowly so she couldn't hear even that slight sound. We didn't move and pressed tightly together and just as tightly against the tree trunk until we were one with it and would be an especially thick tree trunk if Gwen Wooster looked our way.

She didn't see us, though she stood silent and flicked her eyes everywhere, lips pursed, seeking the source of whatever she'd heard. Swayed uneasily on the balls of her feet, ready to run if something came crashing after her. She was on high alert, but she wasn't afraid, just cautious.

We waited until, as a gift from Heaven, a squirrel scampered up to her, stared at her a few seconds, and then went up the tree nearest her, where it stared at her more from a safe distance and chattered noisily to let her know she'd trespassed on its territory. She relaxed, smiled broadly, waved cheerfully at the squirrel, and continued on her way, not looking back. Not seeing us.

We waited until we were sure she was far ahead and then sagged against the tree trunk and breathed deeply and noisily because she was far enough ahead that she wouldn't hear us.

"We are being ridiculous. She won't eat us."

"She might. Besides, this is better than giving her what she wants, which is my life on a platter to be served to the entire world."

"We don't know that, not really. Maybe it wouldn't be that bad."

"And maybe it would be worse."

There was nothing more to say without sounding as if one reporter was dictating our lives. Which she was and we were letting her, which made us a couple of wimps, but we didn't want to admit to that, so we stopped talking and looked around.

"We're not following her any farther."

"She's gotten this far, she'll find her way home."

So we checked the angle of the sun through the foliage and decided we had time for a leisurely stroll through parts of the forest that would circumnavigate the entire area and would take us as far from Gwen Wooster as possible and still get us home before dark. Because she seemed to know the woods well enough to get home on her own.

We both knew the forest well enough to know where to go so we set out without more talk and soon I'd forgotten all about Gwen Wooster as I followed Max through an area of old growth that resembled a church. I'd often found myself there after church in Johns Falls so I could communicate with God without being distracted by people I loved and cherished but who sometimes talked too much.

CHAPTER 17

It was late afternoon when we reached the river and crossed the plank bridge to the park, stopping to enjoy the thundering crash of the waterfall that gave Johns Falls its name. The overspray felt good after our long, hot walk.

I love being in the forest, but I never was a super-woman, and I never push myself physically, plus I'm the least competitive person on the planet. So I wasn't in the best shape, and the cool mist that we walked through was welcome, and the rainbow that appeared whenever the sun shone from the right angle was an added bonus. Max turned all colors as the mist covered him and turned him into a second rainbow.

He, of course, was in good shape and not tired in the least as he turned back to me, bouncing on the balls of his feet like an athletic Jack-in-the-box. "We should wait here. We'll see Gwen Wooster when she comes out of the woods. Then we won't have to worry about her."

I nodded reluctantly. My feet hurt but the guilt trip he was dumping on me was effective. "It's the right thing to do." She was a person, after all, and as such, deserved concern for her safety.

So we dropped to one of the benches the town council had installed, and I pulled my backpack around so I could retrieve the last two bottles of water. We chugged them down and wished there was more but our thirst was slaked enough that we could wait in relative comfort for the nosy reporter to emerge from the forest so we wouldn't have to worry about her any longer than necessary.

I stuck my feet on the end of the bench and wiggled my toes and leaned against Max as we waited for a long time, at least an hour, maybe more, until our thirst couldn't be ignored any longer, when I said hopefully, "Maybe she went some other way."

"There are several paths through the forest. They all lead to town and are easy to follow once you run across them."

"She must have done so. Couldn't miss them, there are so many."

"A few minutes more, then perhaps we'll leave."

So we waited a bit longer, half an hour maybe, before convincing ourselves that Gwen Wooster was alright, but eventually we rose and checked the rainbow that hovered over the waterfall that was as good as a clock because it only appeared when the sun was at the right angle. That rainbow said it was way past midafternoon.

Max actually growled. "I say we forget about Gwen Wooster because she's probably in town."

"She's most likely in her motel room right now with her feet up and a good book in her hands." It was where I'd be if I were her.

Max stared at the waterfall, then at me, then back at the waterfall, judging the time while admiring the colors, and then he nodded in a decisive way. "How about we give up this fruitless nonsense and head for Jerry's?"

"Cappuccino?" My tongue was hanging out and the waterfall just added to my thirst. "Let's go."

We shook off the droplets that in that time had managed to cover us and made our way through the park and then through Johns Falls itself, until we turned in at Jerry's. The lunch crowd was gone and the evening rush hadn't started so it was quiet, with just a few tables full of mostly locals because the true summer rush hadn't yet begun.

We went straight to the only empty table in the middle of the ones filled with people because after the solitude of the forest, for a reason I've never understood because I'm a solitary person, we wanted to be surrounded by humanity, especially by nice people, the kind who asked how we felt instead of how I was mysteriously connected to the forest.

Jerry brought cappuccinos in our own mugs from the shelf on the wall without being asked, so we must have looked pretty desperate. Max brushed off a few twigs, and I tried to smooth my hair, but the expression on Max's face said it wasn't enough. "I'm going to use the restroom."

"Good idea," he murmured and, as I moved away, I looked at the other people's faces and saw what I looked like in their expressions. It's unfair that guys can wear really short hair that goes through anything and looks good.

When I stared in the restroom mirror, I realized that the one thing I'd forgotten to pack that morning was a comb. I did the best I could with my fingers and did what I hoped was a half-way decent job, enough to make me presentable, then I returned and noted that the covert smiles from Jerry's customers had disappeared and Max's expression had turned into one of approval, but all he said was, "Nice."

Good thing I didn't care what most people thought, but I did care what Max thought, so I filed that approving half-smile and whatever mysterious emotion was in those dark eyes at a depth I hadn't been aware I possessed but that warmed me through and through. I shoved the question in my mind as to what this depth was to the back of my mind to study later, then I sat down and gulped my cappuccino because I truly was thirsty. I didn't care if I burned myself in the process.

Bruce, from the grain elevator, shoved his chair away from his table and looked us over. "Been somewhere rough?" We nodded. "Good time of year for being outside. No mosquitoes and I haven't heard of anyone getting wood ticks yet."

Carolyn, recently retired, nodded. "Good time to go hiking if you have the stamina." She looked us over carefully and decided that, yes, that's what we'd been doing. "Now me, I'd stay in my back yard and do nothing at all." Saw our torn clothes and the scratches on our arms and faces. "But I'm curious. Where are there bushes so full of thorns that you came back looking like you lost an encounter with a bear?"

Max and I studied each other. Thought about the butterfly oasis. Knew it should be kept safe from prying eyes. But we also knew that no sane person would attempt the trek we'd just made and, if they did, the butterflies would most likely have moved on by then. "Beyond the new growth. In the big woods. In a clearing. It's pretty, saw some butterflies, but it's nasty walking."

Everyone nodded and turned back to their afternoon treats. No one asked for a more specific description because they were normal, sane people who, after looking us over from head to toe, would never replicate our journey. Carolyn continued the conversation. "You two are the only people I know cray enough to tramp through a thicket of thorns."

Max silently agreed as Bruce picked up the conversation again, sotto voice. "I'll bet my house that my friend Max didn't choose the route. I'll bet he followed Anna."

A chuckle met his words as Jerry took our cups to refill them, shaking his head at how quickly we'd downed his culinary creations, too quickly to enjoy his considerable barista ability. Jerry stared forlornly at the empty bottoms of our mugs as he agreed with the speaker. "Yep, Max has good sense except where Anna is concerned. Which means he followed her." He looked at me with a crooked half-smile. "Anna. Our very own local forest sprite."

"Dryad." Bruce corrected him. "Forest spirits are dryads, not sprites. I heard that somewhere. Can't remember where."

"I'm not a dryad. Or a sprite." My words were automatic, unthinking, and probably a mistake because laughter erupted from every table.

Bruce scratched his head in thought. "Now I remember. That lady reporter – what's her name? – oh, yes, Gwen something-or-other – she knew all about sprites and dryads and stuff like that. She was asking a lot of questions the other day and somehow, in the process, she kind of educated me."

"Questions?" I gulped.

He frowned harder. "Yes. A lot of them, actually." Still harder. "Questions about you now that I think back." He nodded, remembering. "She thinks you're some kind of forest witch. Or sprite. Or dryad. Or something like that."

Everyone laughed, but as they laughed their eyes took in Max and me and our disheveled appearance, until Carolyn asked. "Where'd you say you were in the woods?"

I wiggled uncomfortably and looked to Max for help. He shrugged elaborately. "Here and there. You know, we went for a walk and got semi-lost."

More laughter and someone two tables away said, "Not likely. Not Anna."

Another voice chimed in. "She knows those woods like the back of her hand."

A third asked, "Butterflies, you say? In the forest?"

I was even more uncomfortable, and nothing Max could say would help because they knew me. But butterflies were a diversion and I ran with them. "A lot of butterflies. All colors. Deep in the woods. In a thorn thicket."

Everyone took a moment to digest that information. Then I diverted their attention from me entirely. "Gwen Wooster was there, too. She took a lot of pictures."

"The lady reporter?" I nodded.

A few frowns appeared as everyone looked at each other. Someone checked the time. "Speaking of the reporter, where is she now?"

"I don't know." And I didn't care.

The speaker continued. "She's usually here about now. Getting her free afternoon cappuccino." Because everyone with their own mug got a free cappuccino during the afternoon lull and Gwen Wooster had one.

Max and I looked at one another and knew that we were thinking the same thing. Was the reason we hadn't seen Gwen Wooster exit the forest because she was still there? And if that was the case, was she lost?

I stared at my cappuccino, not wanting to think what I was thinking. That if she was lost, perhaps I was partly to blame because I'd gone into the forest specifically to avoid her and she'd followed me there. If I'd have stayed home, she'd have stayed out of the forest and would be safe.

I couldn't stare at my mug forever. I raised my eyes to Max's and saw that he was thinking the same thing except that the way he shook his head every so slightly said it wasn't my fault and I shouldn't blame myself. But his expression also said that if there was any possibility that Gwen Wooster was lost in the forest then it was our responsibility to find her.

Because we knew where she'd gone. We'd seen her last. We'd have the best chance of locating her. And we couldn't just leave her there.

Max raised his mug and gulped down the last of its contents, and I did the same. Then we grabbed a half dozen cans of pop that I plopped into my backpack and we left Jerry's, waving goodbye to everyone and not saying where we were going, letting them think that we'd simply had enough and were heading home because we didn't want anyone to know that we were returning to the forest to find a potentially lost person..

First, though, we turned towards the motel to see if she was there, hoping she was there while at the same time hoping she wasn't because I didn't want to talk to her and dreaded her seeing me but there was no avoiding that we had to know whether she was safely back. If she was there, we told ourselves, we'd high-tail it away from the motel before she could get a glimpse of us.

The clerk said that Gwen Wooster hadn't returned. He knew because there was an envelope from some newspaper for her and he'd left a note on her door about it and she hadn't come to pick it up so he'd gone to remind her and there'd been no answer to his knock.

We digested that information and then headed for the park where we crossed the plank bridge, but the sun had dropped low enough that there was no rainbow, which meant evening was approaching.

Then we stared at the trees that grew so thick that they seemed like a wall and took deep breaths before plunging into the forest.

CHAPTER 18

It was a lot darker than the last time we'd been under those same trees, which meant it was growing late. Not too much longer and it would be dark. Then there'd be no finding anyone and we'd have to wait for morning. We didn't want to do that, so we picked up the pace and slogged farther, faster, deep into the forest, lifting our feet high so as not to trip over unseen roots because we were in too much of a hurry to choose where to step, an automatic reaction because we'd done this before, though those other times had been more along the line of looking for dogs than a person we didn't particularly like.

"Where would she go?"

"If she's lost she could be anywhere." We sighed, knowing our task was that much harder. Bobby Deal had been following butterflies and that had made finding him easier. Just follow the butterflies. Gwen Wooster was looking for me and I wasn't there any longer, so who knew where she might have gone.

But I had been in the forest and she'd followed me just as I'd followed those butterflies so that must mean something. Furthermore, she'd done quite well. The woman obviously knew how to find her way around.

From traveling the world?

Had she stopped looking for me when she found the butterflies? "Maybe she gave up on me in favor of photographing butterflies." Or had she meandered through the forest in hopes of finding me?

Max shrugged. "I doubt it, but if she did, she went somewhere. What would she do after leaving the butterflies? Where'd she go?"

"Home?" That's where I'd go.

Max nibbled his lower lip. "Suppose she started home. Let's assume she did. We followed her a bit, and she was headed for the river and Johns Falls. But when she heard us, she stopped and looked back."

"She could have thought we were a bear."

"She didn't act afraid, just curious, and then she continued on her way."

"We followed her almost to the edge of the forest. I'm sure she was headed towards Johns Falls. Had to be, town was in a direct line, and she was following that line."

"What if she decided she didn't want to go home until she found you. What if she reached the edge of the forest and turned back to look some more?"

"So we start where we last saw her."

"That's not too far from here."

We picked up the pace even more, coming as close to running as is possible in the forest, and soon we were where we'd last seen her, where she'd heard us and stopped to look back. Where we'd faded into the trees and disappeared because we didn't want her to know we were there.

We looked around. Then we looked more. Then we sagged in defeat. Max kicked a tree root. "Now what?"

I didn't know but we had to do something. Anything. So I pretended to know what I was doing and kind of circled around and checked out the ground without paying attention to what I was doing, hoping for something to catch my eye, but nothing did, so as the minutes passed my movements grew more and more aimless.

Until I spied a footprint in the soft, spongy, earth. I pointed wordlessly and Max joined me. "It was her. Had to be. No one else has been in this area this spring and snow would have eliminated last year's tracks." He slapped me on the back, carefully missing the backpack. "You did it, Anna! You found her tracks. I knew you could. She's right when she says that you have a special ability."

"I'm not a freak." I drew back a little and looked away. Stared at nothing.

He reached for me, but then stopped and let his arm drop without touching me. "Of course not. But you are special, a kind of a miracle worker in the forest, and I'm in awe of your ability." He studied the footprint and then moved in the direction it pointed and excitedly, pointed to a second print. "And now you should be in awe of me too, because I just found another foot print."

I laughed. Max could do that to me. Take away the sting that so often came with comments about my time in the forest, and there had been many such comments over the years, but never by Max, and I was ashamed that I'd doubted him. I touched him and let my hand trail down his arm, and he knew what I was trying to say. His eyes went warm and even darker than usual, and then we both turned to the task at hand.

We were careful. We weren't meandering after

butterflies with more coming along every few minutes so if we lost one there'd be another one soon. This time we were following footprints and couldn't afford to miss a single one.

But the footprints were there. Not every step left an impression but there were enough that, looking hard and following the direction they led, there were enough to know that we were headed the right way. And that way showed that Gwen Wooster was, indeed, lost because the tracks went in a circle, as usually happens when someone is lost in the woods.

We'd find her. We knew it. Going in a circle meant she was nearby. But it was growing late. The sun was still full in the sky but the slant of those rare shafts that found their way through the thick foliage were dropping closer to the western horizon. They were almost horizontal. Soon they would dip below the horizon, and we'd be in the dark.

"Should we continue?" Max looked anxiously at a streak of sunshine that was almost horizontal. We were minutes from dark, and dark came quickly and completely in the forest.

I bit my lip. In fifteen minutes, we'd be unable to see tracks or much of anything. "I think we've got a little longer."

"Not much." His scowl said how late it was.

I stooped low to the ground and inspected the latest footprint. "It's dark at ground level already. Pretty soon we won't see tracks to follow."

"We can keep going until the sun drops below the horizon but as soon as that happens, we make for the river and town." And safety, though he didn't say that because the forest at night was different from during the day. Large predators prowled through the dark. Prey animals moved cautiously and sometimes didn't live to see the next day. And it was easy to get lost, even for someone with unusually good skills.

"Fifteen minutes." I started to shift my backpack but didn't have to because Max grabbed it and slung it over a shoulder. "You've been carrying it long enough."

"It's too small for you."

"I'll manage." So we struck off once more in the general direction of the tracks we'd been following.

And then it happened. The end of our search.

It came with a brightly cheerful yell. "Hi, there, people." We were so startled that we both jumped. Then we looked towards the sound and there was the object of our search. Gwen Wooster. "Just the people I've been looking for, and I've been looking for longer than I care to admit. Most of the day."

"Because you got lost," Max muttered too low for her to hear. "Which happened because you shouldn't have been here in the first place."

But she didn't hear, simply let her smile grow until it dazzled as she strode through the forest towards us, crushing brush and throwing branches every which was in her eagerness to reach us as quickly as possible.

She was in a rush and, though she tried to hide it, she was almost panicky. She'd been lost and we were her saviors and she wasn't about to let us out of her sight until we were safe and sound on the main street of Johns Falls. But I said nothing as she came beside us and reached in a pocket and brought out a small, portable recorder. "Would you mind answering a few questions?"

Really?! The lost woman who'd just been rescued wanted an interview?! But she was a reporter so we shouldn't have been surprised. Max coughed to cover what he was thinking while I swallowed a couple times and shook my head and let he know that an interview should be the last thing on our minds. "It's almost dark and we should get out of the woods as quickly as possible."

The smile grew if such was possible, outshining the last rays of the sun that pinpointed her tall, thin frame like a spotlight, as she chose not give up on a potential interview. A born reporter. "Is it late? I hadn't noticed."

"Oh yes she noticed and was almost in full panic mode," was Max's next muttered comment as he still hid behind his hand and coughed a couple more time to cover his words.

"Why don't we all head for the river?" I suggested it as politely as if we'd met on a street corner instead of in the middle of a primeval forest moments before dark and the dangers that came with it. "We can walk together."

"That would be nice. Companions." She shoved the recorder back into her pocket as she failed to hide her relief at being found and gestured for me to lead the way, all without the smile dimming a single watt.

"Smart woman," Max muttered, looking at the ground so she wouldn't see his lips move. "Pretending she knows where she is, and she's being sooooo polite in letting you take the lead." He snorted quietly, hiding the gesture with a hand. "You should refuse. See what she does. That smile will disappear fast."

But I didn't. Instead I kicked Max gently in the

shins as I passed him and the still smiling Gwen Wooster and headed up our little party of three, taking off at a very fast walk towards the river and civilization because if we almost ran, we might get there before the sun truly sank below the horizon and night fell around us and we started tripping over everything.

But as soon as we reached the river and crossed the plank bridge and could see the buildings of Johns Falls beyond the thicket that separated the river from the town, she whipped out that recorder again and came up beside me. "Now, how about a few questions?"

FLORENCE WITKOP

CHAPTER 19

I sagged and said the truth. "I'm tired." She
moved from one foot to the other, obviously not tired in
the least after a day of hard trekking. Like Max, the
woman was a fitness nut. But I'm not.

She frowned and that frown told me what she was
thinking. I'd eluded her so far but she had me in her
clutches and wasn't about to let go whether I was tired
or not. But she also owed me because I'd found her
when she was lost and that deserved consideration on
her part. What to do?

She figured it out because figuring things out was
included in her job description. Her face brightened
even more if such was possible, with that smile turning
into a blazing spotlight as she asked cunningly, "How
about we adjourn to Jerrys and I treat you two to some
of his famous cappuccino and a dinner of anything on
the menu that your little hearts desire?" I looked at Max
but he studiously looked away. This was my decision
and he wasn't about to interfere. "While we're eating –
after a bit of rest, of course, because we are all a bit
tired – we can talk." She turned that smile full in my
face. "It'll be fun. And interesting. And educational
because you know so much about the forest, and I'd

love to learn."

I wanted to resist but didn't know how because she'd been right when we first met and my mother had taught me to be polite. Besides, I didn't want to admit that I'd been hiding from her, so we slowly made our way back to Jerrys and chose a booth near the back where it was quiet and private and we could talk whether I wanted to or not.

Several patrons, seeing us, nodded and I heard one gentleman say the interesting lady reporter had been looking for Anna and now she'd found her and wasn't that nice? I harrumped as Jerry took our orders while trying not to laugh because he knew how hard I'd been running from Gwen Wooster and he didn't care that I'd been trapped since we ended up at his place and he was getting business.

I glared at him, and silently told him not to listen in on the conversation, but something about his expression said he'd do as he pleased in that regard, which meant that of course he'd listen but he'd never share what he heard because he has standards.

As we waited for our food, Gwen Wooster flipped out her recorder, frowned a moment as she thought how to get started, then looked straight at me and asked, "Are you a witch? Sprite? Dryad? Which?"

"Huh?" My mouth dropped a mile. "No, no, no! None of those things."

"Then what are you? What kind of supernatural ability do you posses that kicks into play whenever you enter the forest?" She leaned across the table the better to see and hear my answers, holding her recorder like a wand. "And is it any forest you are in or just this one where you grew up? And how did it start? Were you a kid or an adult when you first realized you have special powers? And --- and – and –"

My mouth stayed wide enough open that a dozen flies could have entered if any had been around as I tried to take in what she was asking. Yes, I knew she wanted a story about my ability to find my way in the forest, but this was ridiculous. I looked to Max for help and then to Jerry, who was bringing plates heaped with spaghetti, but neither of them came to my rescue. In fact they both sort of leaned back to better hear my answers.

"Do you do anything special to invoke your powers?" She hardly stopped for breath. "An incantation of some kind? A spell you weave? Do you draw a pentagram before entering the forest?" At my look of horror, she asked, "Do you pray?"

I shook my head, unable to speak, as Max and Jerry turned red from their efforts to not laugh. "None of those things. Nothing at all." Maybe I'd pray if I heard what sounded like a large animal coming my way, but I wasn't about to tell her so for fear she'd interpret it wrong. Instead I raised my hands and tried to protect myself from the wall of words, but it didn't work, the words didn't stop.

"Does anyone else in your family have this ability?" I shook my head no, and she spoke into her recorder to give voice to my answer. "What do they think of it? Did they treat you differently once it manifested?"

"Manifested? Ability?" My voice choked. I almost couldn't speak. I took a deep breath and thought what to say. How to stop this onslaught. I had to say something that would make her stop. "I hate to disappoint you, Ms. Wooster, but I don't have any special ability, and I don't do anything out of the ordinary when I go for a walk in the woods. I just go for a walk."

She leaned back in her chair and stared at me, not believing my heartfelt speech, while Jerry and Max watched us both with that expression guys wear while watching a fascinating guy-type movie with cowboys or spies or green aliens that are about to go to war with each other. Breathless. And Gwen Wooster just kept staring in that unblinking way.

Until her eyes narrowed and she leaned closer, hunching still farther over the table and our partially eaten dinner. We were inches apart. Eyeball to eyeball. I wanted to back off but didn't because something about her, some charisma, kept me rooted to the spot.

She blinked. "I believe you." Then she settled back into her chair on the other side of the table while continuing to stare at me, holding me in thrall. "I truly believe that you don't know what you do even as you do it." She nodded to herself. "That's how it is with all the greatest witches – warlocks – dryads – with all beings that are beyond the normal world. It comes so naturally that you don't realize what you're doing."

I gagged and opened my mouth to protest but snapped it shut again as I realized that I didn't have the slightest idea how to refute her words because no matter what I said, my words would be used against me, as she nodded abruptly and said, "That'll make the story harder to write but I'll manage. I promise that it'll be great. I've done it before, written a full story from a few bare-bones facts, and this story will be my crowning glory. My best."

"I'm not special. I'm not a story." I felt myself

sliding down in my chair, trying to disappear into the floor, but it didn't work.

"Oh but you are. You are a story because everyone is a story, though some are more interesting than others and you, my dear, are fascinating." She stared at me with those mesmerizing eyes as if we were the only people in the room. "When did it start, that's the first thing I want to know. Need to know for the story. You and the forest. When was the first time? Did something happen to make you realize what you are?"

The question was so unexpected that I couldn't hide my expression, and the instant she saw it she seized upon my slip. "I knew it! Something happened! It's almost always that way." She eased back a bit, relaxing, eager for a story. "So tell me about it. Were you alone or with someone? Did the trees speak to you? How did you know? Were you afraid? What happened, anyway? Don't keep me in suspense, girl."

I don't know how she did it. Maybe it was her expression, so knowing, so mesmerizing. For whatever reason, I found myself telling her about that first time when I was young and got lost in the forest. As I spoke, she nodded and though I didn't realize it at the time she recorded everything.

When I came back to reality and saw the recorder, I spoke in a squeaky voice. "I'm not a freak. Please don't make me a freak."

She softened and reached out and lay a hand on mine. It was warm and comforting. "Don't worry, child, I'll do right by you. When I'm done with this story, you'll be a rose among thorns and will come across as absolutely wonderful, all pretty and feminine and sweet and innocent and beautiful. And special as heck."

She touched my cheek, and her hand was caring. "Because you are wonderful, did you know that?" Her touch was light and I could see in her eyes that the story was already written in her mind and, somehow, in those eyes I knew that she was truly sympathetic and would say only nice things. "You are a true child of nature. A wonder."

Then the spell she'd had me in broke and I remembered that she was a reporter. Yikes! I looked to Max and Jerry for help but they were still in thrall as much as I'd been and now were only able to stare at Gwen Wooster with blank expressions.

I'd given her the interview she'd been after for so long, and she had it all down in her recorder, and it was too late to take anything back. She clicked the recorder off, shoved it in a pocket, and started to rise, but Max caught her sleeve and stopped her.

She looked a question at him and he cleared his throat and managed to find his voice, coming out of the spell she'd had us all under. "She's completely normal, Ms. Wooster, and your article had better say so."

"Of course she is." Gwen Wooster gently brushed Max's hand away and dropped a few bills on the table, way more than the cost of the meal. "She's a totally normal and very nice young lady who happens to have a special ability that most of us don't have and that ability makes her --- interesting."

"You can't –" Max began. "You mustn't –" The Max of old still trying to protect me from the bullies of the world.

Gwen Wooster shushed him with an elegant wave of one of her long, slender hands, and then she once again turned on that thousand-watt smile that had made the forest day-bright and now sent a thousand shards of light through Jerrys. "If you're concerned that I'm going to turn our wonderful Anna into a freak, don't worry. I'd never do that. She's a lovely young woman and my story will make that abundantly clear."

She sauntered towards the door, stopping just long enough to pick up her mug from the shelf on the wall because she wouldn't be back. She had her story and was on her way to other things. "I'm sure you'll see the piece when it's published. You'll love it, and that's a promise." Then she disappeared through the door and from Johns Falls and my life.

"Well!" Jerry brought us fresh cappuccinos while shaking his head until I wondered if he also was having a difficult time getting past the spell Gwen Wooster had cast. "There should be cake because this is a celebration." He thought a moment, then disappeared into the kitchen and returned with a box of cupcakes, goodness knows where they came from because he doesn't serve cupcakes, but of course they were wonderful, creative, and delicious.

He maneuvered expertly among the tables with that platter of cupcakes in one hand, dropping them onto tables as he went, waving away attempts on the part of his customers to pay. "Not today. This is a party."

An elderly man peeled the paper from his double-chocolate cupcake. "A goodbye party, I believe." He harrumped a couple times.

Jerry nodded. "Goodbye to Gwen Wooster, who is a semi-nice lady." He deposited a half dozen cupcakes on a table for the women's club that was meeting there and continued. "But she does have a one-track mind, and tact isn't her strong suit, and for a while there I thought she was a bulldozer on track to flatten Anna." Laughter greeted him as various customers sampled various cupcakes and nodded approval.

One elderly woman said, "No one had better mistreat our Anna," while closing her eyes in ecstasy over a maraschino cherry cupcake with pink frosting.

The man across from her said, "Just 'cause Anna can find her way through the woods without tripping over her feet is no reason to plaster her all over some newspaper," as he sampled a double chocolate cupcake topped with peanut butter frosting.

"Anna is good in the forest," a third patron said. "Can't argue with that. She's a real pathfinder. Found my dog when he disappeared and I thought the wolves had got him. Turned out he was playing with a skunk." The speaker shook his head dolefully. "It was a while before we let him in the house, and I think Anna held her nose the whole time she was bringing him home."

More laughter and then, as customers noticed the time, one table after another emptied, and the residents of Johns Falls went about their business, and when Max and I tossed our crumbled cupcake papers into the trash and exited Jerrys place with clouds obscuring both the moon and stars, dark had settled over the town like a down-filled quilt.

"Glad we got out of the forest while it was still light."

"We'd have managed no matter the time." I said the words without thinking.

Max stopped and looked long at me. "*You'd* have managed because that guy was right when he called you a pathfinder. If I was alone in the woods, I'd have had to camp overnight."

"Naaa." I punched him in the shoulder and took back my backpack that was still slung over one shoulder. "You'd have been home in no time because I'd have saved you."

He turned towards me. Grinned. Made sure the backpack was on right. Stopped grinning and simply looked at me. Moved from one foot to the other. Opened his mouth to say something. And then turned and strode away, disappearing into the dark.

I went home, fed Casey, emptied the backpack, and stood in the doorway and looked out over my back yard and beyond to mentally picture the forest that rose up so quickly past the edge of town. The forest that was now a big deal to at least one reporter. The forest I loved and where I felt completely at home.

It was something I did often, picturing the forest in my mind, especially if I was upset about something. So now, once again, I closed my eyes to see that pristine place and find the peace that it always brought. But, for the first time ever, no forest filled my mind.

Instead I saw Max, tall and blocky and totally male, with dark eyes that I usually read as easily as I read a book but that had said things I couldn't comprehend during those last few moments before he left. Things I wished I'd understood but hadn't.

Why did I see Max instead of the forest when all that had happened was that our glances had met? I didn't have a clue. But somehow, for some unknown reason, I felt warmer, closer, happier from that look than I'd ever felt from walking in the forest.

CHAPTER 20

That happy moment didn't last. Oh, it did for a while. I went back to staring at my computer on behalf of Hollander and Company while trying to convince Casey that I wasn't ignoring him. How did Max manage with two dogs who thought their owner should spend all of his time with them? I gave the computer keys a few viscous swipes as I promised myself that next time Max and I got together, I'd ask. I might be good in the forest, but Max was the dog whisperer.

So, all in all, things were quiet and normal and comfortable. Until Gwen Wooster's story was published, and my world fell apart.

No one in Johns Falls got the magazine it was in so we didn't know it had happened. And it started innocuously enough. A nice, elderly man who was passing through Johns Falls stopped at Jerry's for coffee and, after glancing around, asked if this was where Anna something-or-other lived. Then he enlarged on that. "You know, the girl who knows her way through the worst the north woods can come up with. The tree person. The dryad, or something similar." He wrinkled his forehead with effort.

Jerry, who'd been on his way to the kitchen, snapped around. "What did you say?"

The man waved a hand in the air. "I don't recall the exact phrase, but it was in that magazine. You know, the one about interesting people. The one that tells all about a person, with lots of pictures." He looked over the café. "I didn't pay that much attention to where the tree lady was from, but it was a great story, and when I saw the sign on the edge of town I thought it sounded like the place where she lives."

Jerry studied the floor. "Anna, huh? That's a common name."

"It was a common name, and I can't remember her surname. But I'm sure she's from somewhere in this area, and she found that little boy who was lost a while back. The one the dogs saved from hypothermia." He brightened. "That was in all the papers, I believe, though I don't recall seeing anything about this Anna at the time." He frowned again, momentarily. "The Anna thing came later, when that lady reporter wrote a story about her."

He snapped his fingers. "Reilly, that's her last name. I remember it now. Anna Reilly." He looked at Jerry. "Does she live around here?"

Jerry's face went all studious before going totally blank. "Can't say. Maybe you should ask at the next town over."

The man grabbed his coffee in a to-go Styrofoam cup and dropped money on the counter. "It's not that important. I probably got everything wrong, anyway. It was just that Johns Falls sounded familiar, and it seemed to be in connection with that Anna Reilly who can find her way through the thickest forest in no time because she's – special."

He turned to go. "Special, that's what the article said. Born with a gift, it said. Or was given a gift by the forest itself." He snorted. "As if forests were people, going around giving things away."

He reached the door but turned back before leaving. "The article said she has a bond with the forest that's beyond the comprehension of us run-of-the-mill people." He shook his head as he pushed into the bright day. "Wish I had something special. She's a lucky woman." And he was gone.

Jerry told me about his visitor the very next day when I stopped by after my usual conference with the Hollander and Company manager. "No one else has asked about you, though, and I didn't let on that you live in Johns Falls so he's not telling anyone." He filled the cup I'd brought from its place on the wall. "So maybe it was a one-off thing."

It wasn't. The next person was another reporter, a young guy just out of college and looking to expand his reportorial skills. "Where's the tree whisperer?" he asked everyone he met, collaring people on street corners and in shops. "She lives around here, and I want to meet her." He smiled every time, I was told, while almost pinning people to the nearest building. "I'll make her famous, unlike that first reporter who beat around the bush when it came to her extraordinary abilities." He'd shove them against whatever wall was easily available and lean in close to get their answers and wouldn't let them up until he was convinced that they knew nothing.

Fortunately for me Johns Falls residents are good liars. They can increase the size of a recently caught fish exponentially without cracking a smile and exaggerate the danger of a bear encounter without appearing to fabricate a thing. Compared to those things, making one resident disappear was easy. So the reporter eventually left and I was free to continue going about my life in peace.

Problem was, not everyone was easy to discourage and Gwen Wooster had included my picture in her article. How she got it I never knew, but when Max finally got around to getting the magazine the article was in, there I was in full color and spread all across four pages, with the forest in the background and surrounded by thousands of butterflies.

She must have found me in the forest before I realized she was there and had taken pictures. All those pictures of butterflies had been extra, and I now suspected she'd photo-shopped many of them into the magazine picture to make it appear that I'd called them to that spot.

"Maybe this'll be the end of it," Max said sympathetically as we spread the magazine over his table and examined each picture carefully. There were a lot of them and the article itself was extensive and took up a large portion of the magazine. There was no way anyone reading it could miss learning a lot about me, whether that information was accurate or not.

Max tried to be upbeat. "The magazine is a couple weeks old. Surely other, more interesting, things have been written since then." He touched my shoulder gently. "People will forget."

People didn't forget. Instead, they got worse. A young couple with a cute, tubby toddler wanted me to teach their child how to navigate the forest, after which they planned on building a house there. They wanted my imprint on their child so as not to worry about him getting lost. They were very angry when I refused. As they stormed off, they said I didn't care if children got lost or worse.

Jerry clucked a few times after politely shooing such people from his café. "I'm afraid you're in for it, Anna and that this is just the beginning."

He was right. I soon lost track of the people who drove to Johns Falls and asked for me. It didn't matter that everyone I knew said they didn't know me, or that I'd gone on a trip, or was in the hospital, or whatever excuse they could come up with to send the 'Anna seekers' as they came to be called, on their way. Because Johns Falls is a small town, tiny really, and anyone with an ounce of imagination could find my rented house that was smack dab in the center of town. But they didn't.

So I took to hiding in the house. I got a lot of work done for Hollander and Company, though Casey couldn't understand why I didn't throw his ball across the back yard any more, not dreaming that it was because I didn't like people hanging over the fence to better take my picture.

One semi-good thing happened. I was on the main street of town getting groceries, and I was in full disguise in sunglasses and a long-sleeved shirt with a baseball cap hiding my hair and lime green pants and bright pink sneakers that screamed to everyone who knew about such things that I was a tourist. Occasionally my disguise worked. More often it didn't but it worked enough that I could do essential shopping.

"Oh, Anna!" Someone tugged at my arm. I debated

whether to make a break for it or try to bluff my way out but, unfortunately whomever was pulling me around knew that I was me. So I tamped down my dread, tried out a smile, and turned to the speaker. And gaped. "Gwen Wooster!"

"I'm so sorry, Anna." She, too, wore sunglasses and a baseball cap, but hers was red, white, and blue and the rest of her outfit tagged her as someone who knew what to wear in a small town in northern Minnesota. Jeans, a tee shirt and a pair of sneakers that no longer looked new because a dash of mud is required on shoes in rural areas. She learned fast. "I never dreamed the story would go over so hugely." She looked truly contrite. Was she? I doubted it. "It grew legs and normally that's good, wonderful, for a reporter's career. But I know what it must be doing to you personally."

She stepped back and looked me up and down. "And I was right because you're in disguise." A line appeared between her eyebrows. "Oh dear."

I didn't know what to do. I'd developed a hearty dislike for the woman and here she was being nice and seeming to mean it. I returned the favor, though I was dubious of her real feelings. "It's okay. I'm surviving."

Her eyebrows rose, and she said dryly, "I doubt that."

At that moment, a young woman with long hair and a longer dress came up to us. "You're Anna Reilly, aren't you?" A camera appeared in her hands from nowhere and she somehow shoved Gwen Wooster aside as she sidled up to me, throwing an arm around my neck and almost choking me while handing Gwen her camera. "Would you take our picture? I can't believe I'm actually talking to Anna Reilly, the only living forest dryad in the country."

"The what?" I sputtered.

Gwen Wooster moved and somehow wedged her body between the woman and me, shaking her head and saying with all the faux honesty in the world, "Sorry, dear, but this is my daughter. Bonnie Wooster." She pretended to inspect me through her sunglasses. "Yes, I suppose she does resemble that dryad person, but I can assure you the resemblance is superficial because I know Anna Reilly, and if you should meet her in person you'll see the difference instantly." And she dared the young woman to contradict her.

The woman sighed and put her camera away. "I did so want to see her." Adding wistfully, "I've never met a dryad."

Gwen Wooster, bless her heart, patted the woman on the shoulder and said, "I believe I saw her just a few minutes ago. She was heading for the park by the waterfall. If you run, you might catch her before she leaves."

The woman turned on her heel and was gone, and Gwen Wooster looked at me with raised eyebrows. "How'd I do? Think she bought it?"

I giggled. Never thought I'd giggle around Gwen Wooster but it happened. "Totally, and thank you."

"It's the least I can do, and I'll keep it up as long as necessary." She stared beyond me, to the town of Johns Falls and the forest that began at the edge of the last street. "As long as I can." Then she did something that made me believe her. She reached into the huge purse that functioned as both purse and carry-all for everything a reporter could want and pulled out her mug. "I'm on my way to Jerrys, and I hope he'll let me replace my mug instead of running me out of town."

Jerry run someone out of town? Never happen. "He'll be glad to see you and your mug." Then what she'd said penetrated. "Have you ever been run out of a town?" Because she was a reporter and I suspected she was more persistent than most.

"Many times," was her dry answer. "In fact, I've been run out of some of the most exclusive establishments in the world." She wrapped an arm loosely around my shoulders. "But for now I'm here to protect a very nice, young lady who happens to know her way around the forest. Because I have ethics."

"Will you write a story about that – about you protecting me – when you leave?"

Her reply proved that I was getting to know her. "Of course I will, and it'll be great. I'll be a heroine." With which she half shoved, half dragged me towards Jerrys, where she pushed aside a couple of mugs to make room for hers on the wall shelf, and then she bought us each a cappuccino with double whipping cream.

CHAPTER 21

After that day, however, I made sure not to be too friendly with Gwen Wooster and, since she seemed to frequent Jerrys where the entire town of Johns Falls decided that they loved her unreservedly because she was protecting me while being the epitome of charisma, I headed to Max's place when I felt the need to socialize. Since Max makes the best omelets ever, I cunningly timed my trips for early mornings, so that Casey and I arrived just in time for breakfast and conversation.

At first he thought I was there because I wanted something because that was how things had worked between us for years. He gave and I got. But eventually he figured out that this time was different, and I was seeing him to avoid something. Or someone. And he got it out of me. "So who or what is the horror you don't want to face and are using me to shield you from?"

I looked away and made a big deal of enjoying eggs with sweet peppers and tomatoes and several other things wrapped inside that I didn't recognize but that tasted wonderful as I avoided replying.

He refused to be sidetracked. "Really Anna, what

makes you think you can fool me? We've been friends since Kindergarten. So what's with this sudden love for omelets?"

I gave up. Sighed. Thunked my head on the table a couple of time and told him. "Gwen Wooster is back in town."

He dropped into the chair opposite me and stared, open-mouthed. "I thought she was gone for good." His face scrunched. "She took her mug."

"She brought it back." I raised back to a normal sitting position and took a couple more bites of omelet. It was great so I took a couple more before continuing. "She's sorry for the commotion her article caused."

Max harrumped. "I'll bet her bank statement says otherwise."

I agreed wholeheartedly, but she'd seemed genuinely sorry when we spoke. "She says she's here to run interference with anyone who wants to upend my life."

Another harrumph. "That would include her, and she's done a good job of it if your presence at my breakfast table is any indication."

He slapped another helping of omelet on my plate and dropped the remainder of his creation onto his own, put the pan back on the stove, and proceeded to eat with gusto because he likes his own omelets, which shows what good taste he has. "Though, now that I think about it, maybe I should thank her because I haven't seen you much lately and it's kind of nice to see you again. It's like old times, like when we were kids and you followed me like a puppy dog and waited for me to rescue you."

It was my turn to harrumph a couple times. "Not

very often. Besides, who's the pathfinder in this scenario? Me, that's who." After scarfing down most of the omelet on my plate so I'd be sure to have it eaten if he threw me out for being self-aggrandizing, I waved my fork and continued. "Remember Maxwell, I am the one with the wonderful forest-type skills. I'm the one who can rescue people, including yours truly, if you should ever get lost in the forest. I'm the one who –"

He pushed back from the table, having finished his own breakfast, and plunked his dishes in the dishwasher. "Looks to me like you're an out-of-shape female who needs a big, strong guy to break trail for her, no matter that you know where the trail goes. So the way I see things, you need me more than I need you because you can't do it alone." Then he shut the dishwasher and turned it on, and then he leaned against it, watching me and waiting for me to say something because he knew I would because I always do.

But I didn't because, just like that, in the instant between him putting his dishes in the dishwasher and him leaning against it, everything changed. My whole outlook on life was tilted one hundred and eighty degrees, and it happened while nothing happened other than that he turned and leaned against the dishwasher.

Looking at his blocky form draped over that dishwasher in jeans that had seen better days and wouldn't protect him from nasty thorns if we went for a walk in the forest, and the worn shirt that clung to his shoulders, while feeling the strength of those dark, dark eyes that slanted down towards me and remembering the heat of the body that had kept me warm during many winter outings, I couldn't joke any longer. Couldn't if I'd wanted to.

And I realized right then and there that I was in love with Max. Max!!! My childhood friend, the guy I'd never in a million years have expected to have romantic feelings for.

I was stunned. Speechless. Literally unable to say a word.

But I couldn't just sit there like an idiot. We were in the midst of a conversation and I had to say something, so I said the first thing that came into my head. The only thing I could think of that was safe and would hold his attention while I got control of myself.

I continued the story I'd told him of that time in the forest when I was a child that had opened something in me – some ability? – that had grown over time instead of diminishing. I told him, and he listened intently and didn't realize that I was stumbling around trying to speak clearly. I don't think he even blinked.

And then I said – because it was true but I'd never told anyone before and wouldn't now if the occasion wasn't so urgent -- "I believe that I do have an affinity with the forest. An ability that's beyond normal." Then, realizing what I'd just said and how ridiculous it sounded, I amended my statement. "Maybe I do."

Before he could shut his mouth and say anything about my truly bizarre belief, a commotion outside drew our attention. The three dogs barked loudly and we went to the window to check things out.

A youngish woman in a clingy, frothy dress with a haircut that could have been done with a lawnmower but had probably cost a month's pay was trying to placate the dogs that refused to let her walk up to the door, tossing them tiny pieces of beef jerky with every step they allowed.

Max whispered, though it was doubtful she could hear. "I'll have to talk to those dogs. They shouldn't succumb to bribes."

"Who is she?"

"How should I know?" His gaze went over her somewhat other-worldly appearance, and his eyebrows rose. "Really, Anna, where would I meet someone like that and why would I want to? I don't think she lives in Johns Falls because, if she did, we'd have heard about her, constantly, by everyone who believes people should be normal." He pointed. "Look at that dress. Is she wearing curtains?"

I giggled, glad for the relief. I was still reeling from realizing that I was in love and needed a break from the havoc my body was experiencing. "It's kind of cute."

He peered closer from behind the blinds. "I'll get rid of her while you hide."

I did as he said and, shortly, she was gone and he returned. "She didn't know you were here but she was looking for you and somehow she learned that we're friends and thought that she could get to you through me."

"Thanks for sending her away." I wanted to hug him but wasn't sure I should because we weren't the hugging kind of friends and that was a good thing because, having just figured out that I was in love with him, I wasn't sure what would happen if we were.

The next morning, after we'd finished breakfast and were discussing world events with our feet on Max's coffee table and our heads on the back of his couch, there was a knock on his door. When he answered, something about his voice told me that I'd best disappear, so I quickly slipped into his bedroom and pulled the drapes closed and shut the door.

He found me later. "I sent them away but this is getting ridiculous."

"Gwen Wooster said she'd run interference."

"Gwen Wooster doesn't know this town – or you – well enough to keep the hoards from running over you like a road grader."

I thought over what he'd said. "You shouldn't have to put up with this either because I have a perfectly good house, and I can lock my doors and pull my drapes and wait it out there just as easily as here. Nothing lasts forever and, eventually, all these people will stop coming." I waved a hand in the air. "It's just a magazine article, and I'm just a person who likes to walk in the forest."

"And always knows where she is, and finds lost boys, and is a local legend, and that's different. Unique. Special." He came close and touched my shoulder, sending shock waves through my body that I hoped he didn't notice. "But I have an idea for today."

"What?"

He held up a finger. "Everyone is looking for you because you are the forest sprite and, in a way, that's exactly what you are. So, Miss Forest Sprite, why don't we take the dogs and go for a walk in the forest? We can spend a whole day so deep in the woods that no one will ever find us, and we won't return until dark, and then you can stay at my place if you want, and I'll barricade the doors against any incursions."

It was the perfect idea. I simply nodded agreement, and we packed a few things like mosquito repellant and water for us and the dogs and sandwiches and cookies that were almost stale so had to be eaten soon, and tied jackets around our waists in case it grew cool before we returned, and we stepped out of his yard and into the forest.

CHAPTER 22

The moment we stepped into the forest I knew Max's instinct was right, and I suspected I wasn't the only one who needed the peace of the woods. Being in love with Max had made me way more sensitive to him than I'd ever have believed possible. I now noticed how he walked whether I wanted to or not. What he watched. How he smiled or frowned as we passed along the faint game trails that were like highways to us both. And, oddly enough, I was also getting a feel for what was going on inside of him. Sort of.

Not entirely because there was still a part of him that I couldn't know, but up to the instant I hit that part I could read him pretty well. When we were kids, he'd been the one who knew what I was thinking before I knew it myself. But now I knew – absolutely *knew* – that, for some reason, this trek was exactly what he needed, and he needed it as much as I did.

We trekked far into the forest, silent but companionable, as the stress of the last days and weeks fell away, and we both agreed that this was exactly what we needed.

As we walked, the trees grew larger and taller until we were in an area that hadn't been logged for more years than we'd been alive. I'd been there many years earlier and thought that I remembered a place of great beauty and suddenly, as we walked, I wanted to show Max that special place just because it was lovely, and I wanted to share that with the man I loved even though he'd never know why.

So I gradually veered from the usual path and into an area we'd never been together. Max paused once and gave me an inquiring look, but then turned back to the trail because he knew I had someplace specific in mind. He knew by my expression that we'd end up someplace beautiful because that's what was behind this foray. Quiet, and peace, and the forest we both knew intimately, and together those things melded into simple beauty.

And so we walked until we reached my special place, and then I stopped and dropped my backpack onto the ground. I turned to Max and let him see where I'd brought him, and he smiled, not saying anything because he didn't have to. He knew why we'd come here, and he approved.

"We didn't bring bathing suits," was all he said finally, moving closer to the small pond formed by the backwater eddy of a tiny creek that meandered beneath the trees. He tipped his head to one side, and said, "And we don't need them. Our clothes will dry when we're done."

And so they would, as all kids know. Take your shoes off and walk into and out of the water and don't worry about clothes because they dry quickly in the summer air. It had been years since we'd done that, but we knew the drill.

"If the water's warm enough for swimming. It's

early in the year, so it might be like ice."

"It gets enough sun that it could be warm."

"One way to find out." Max stooped to the tiny pond and stuck a hand in, moved it about a bit, then nodded. "It's cool, but not cold. We won't stay in long, but I'm all for a brief dip."

So we took off our shoes, stripped to our jeans and shirts and, hands held to give each other courage to step into the cool water, we waded in. Shivered. Waded further. Shivered more. And dropped until we were submerged and then came up quickly, still shivering but less so, and shook our hair until we could see again. We turned our faces up to that sliver of sun and let it warm us until we adjusted to the water. Then we let go of each other's hands and waded back and forth, it being too shallow for swimming.

"The current is stronger than I expected." It pressed my jeans against my body on one side and ballooned them away on the other.

Max examined the main body of the creek. "I think it's deeper than it looks in the main body of the creek where there's current. That explains the current."

"How deep is it?" I was curious. "Enough that we can swim?" I moved towards the creek itself, stepping cautiously as I left the tiny pond, and the water deepened. "Maybe we can swim after all." I took another step. Then another.

Then everything went black.

When the world returned, I was lying on the bank with Max staring down at me. To be truthful, I *thought* he was staring down at me but everything was so woozy that I wasn't sure of anything.

I did hear his voice. "A log hit you."

"Log?" I was still woozy. "What log? It's a creek, not a river. Too tiny for logs."

"Big enough, and it came around the bend fast in that current. That's why you didn't see it." His eyebrows furrowed in concern. "Are you okay?" He held up a hand. "How many fingers?"

I tried to count. Couldn't. "Several."

His face went gray. "I've got to get you back to Johns Falls. To a doctor."

I tried to roll onto my side and couldn't. "No need. I just want to take a nap. Right here. The sun is warm, it'll be fine." And I tried to roll again and once more I failed, so I looked up at him. Both of him because there were two Max's peering down at me. "Will you help? It seems I'm a bit lazy at the moment." And I tried again. And failed again.

"No nap for you." His expression hardened. "Not now, not until you've had X-rays, and that means I must get you home." He looked away from me. At the forest. At the sun. At everything. And then he looked back, and he was even grayer than before. "Where are we, Anna? I'll carry you, but I don't know where we are, not exactly. Can you direct us back home?"

I waved an arm. Tried to wave and failed as I'd failed to roll over. "Sure. Nothing to it. I can find my way anywhere. Any time, no problem, but we're here to swim, and we haven't done that yet, not really, not enough." I struggled to sit up so we could go back in the creek, but my muscles were spaghetti. "If you'll just help me sit up, then we can go swimming, and it'll be fun."

One very strong arm came beneath my shoulders, and he pulled me to a sitting position. The world went crazy, and I almost barfed. "Hold it a sec, Max, I seem to be a little dizzy. No big deal, but maybe in a second or two I'll be fine." And I tried to focus and eventually managed. Sort of.

Then he pulled me all the way upright and suddenly, without me knowing how it happened, I was slung over his shoulder like a sack of potatoes, and he was headed away from the creek. After all the work I'd gone to so we could go for a swim, he was headed in the wrong direction. "Hey, Max. The creek is back there."

"We're going home, Anna." And, with me over his shoulder, he plunged into the forest. "If you can get us there."

How dare he end our little jaunt before I was ready! "Not going to happen, Max. Not until we've swum long enough that we're both blocks of ice."

"Where, Anna? Which way is home?"

"I won't say. Not fair that we don't get our swim."

He sighed and stopped long enough to stare at the trees around us. "I'll get us home, Anna. I'll do it so don't you worry about a thing. I'll get you the help you need."

"Then you'll do it without me because I want to go swimming. Or to sleep. Don't know why I'm tired, but I could use a nap. So maybe I'll go to sleep." I giggled.

"Please, Anna, don't go to sleep."

His words penetrated the fog that was growing deeper around me. Max would take care of me. I'd just recently figured out that I loved him. Maybe this wasn't love in return, but it was close, and I held that fact next to my heart. And I said, "I love you, Maxwell. Just thought I'd let you know."

He stopped. The rocking motion of his progress through the trees stopped, and everything went still, and all I knew was the feel of him next to me and the ever present sounds of the forest and the smell of the fecund earth and the warmth of the day even though we were too deep in the woods for the sun's rays to penetrate. "I love you too, Anna, though I doubt you'll remember that fact."

He hoisted me higher on his shoulder, and I wondered if this what potatoes felt like when they were being loaded, and I giggled again. "I'll remember. Forever."

"But first we've got to get home. I think I remember how we got here, but if you'd point the way, it would be helpful."

"Do you love me?" I was having fun. "Say it again, and I'll tell you the way home." I thought over what we'd been talking about – love – and I giggled again. "Because love trumps swimming. I guess."

"Yes it does. Love trumps everything, Anna, and if you'll tell me how to get us home, I'll be forever grateful."

I looked around. Simple. "Any idiot knows where we are. So any idiot can find the way home." I sighed and closed my eyes and wanted to go to sleep, but Max had said not to sleep and since he'd said he loved me, I should do what he asked. It was little enough, I decided.

So I told him where we were and how to get from that place to Johns Falls. And he started moving again, slow and steady, walking as carefully as possible so as not to jar me, and I felt his body next to mine and was happy and decided not to take that nap after all because if I was asleep, I'd not feel that closeness.

And so we went for the longest time. Until I heard the sound of the waterfall that meant we were home, and we emerged from the forest and Max carefully, as if I was delicate, turned me from his shoulder to the ground and peered at me anxiously. "We're here. Can you walk? Are you awake?"

"Sure." I took a step and crumpled and only his arm beneath my shoulder kept me from pitching into the river and the foam from the falls.

"Don't worry, Anna, I'll carry you." A sigh came from him. "I just thought that if you could walk, we'd be less noticeable. So prepare for a parade."

I giggled, wondering in some corner of my mind why I was giggling so much lately, then decided it didn't matter because giggling was a sign of happiness and so should be encouraged. With which I giggled again. "That's okay Max. I like parades."

A low sound from Max said he didn't feel the same, but as I was scooped into his arms and felt more than saw us cross the bridge to the park and then the town of Johns Falls, I didn't care because I was content.

And, yes, we did become a parade as people saw us and came running, and then there were cell phones clicking as pictures were taken, and I thought I heard several tourists saying things about the forest spirit being hurt and needing medical help, and then we were in the clinic, and everything went black once again.

CHAPTER 23

This time, when I woke, I had the worst headache of my life and only Max staring down at me made life bearable. "What happened?"

"We were swimming. You were hit by a floating log. You have a concussion. You'll be fine but you need rest. A lot of rest."

"I don't remember."

"Nothing? You don't remember anything?"

"Just that I wanted to swim. After that, nothing."

Then I blinked and said a few words and was amazed that they were slurred but Max got the gist of them anyway and smiled.

I loved that smile. I loved Max. And, oh my goodness, what had I said while we were in the forest? Had I said something I wished I'd not said? I couldn't remember, but had the thought somewhere deep in me that I might have. Had I admitted that I loved Max? I hoped not but the words 'I love you' kept popping into my mind as I recalled our journey home.

"Did I say anything --- foolish?"

His smile broadened. "Not a thing. Nothing foolish at all."

I didn't believe him. I stared at him as hard as my

headache allowed, which wasn't very hard. "If I did say something stupid – anything -- just ignore it, huh? Because I wasn't in my right mind, so whatever I said doesn't count."

His smile dimmed. "Okay. Whatever you want." It dimmed a bit more as he licked his lips as if trying to decide what to say next, and what he said was, "You weren't in your right mind, so I'll forget what we talked about."

"Good." I closed my eyes against the pain and the bright day. "Now I'd like to sleep if it's okay with you."

"Sure. Anything. I'll go now." But, before he left, as I closed my eyes my eyes, I was sure that I felt a butterfly kiss on my forehead. A few of them. Several, in fact, and I slept better for having them.

When I awoke, time had passed. I didn't know how I knew that beyond the way I felt, which was much better. As I looked around the room and actually focused on things, a nurse wandered past the door. Stopped. Noticed I was awake and came in. "Hi."

I said, 'hi' back, and she noted that on a clipboard. "Yes, I'm awake and I can actually see things." I mentally checked my body. "And my headache is not as bad as it was."

"Great. That means you're improving. You were a mess when that nice young man brought you in though anyone would be a mess with all those people who were following you."

"People followed me?"

"Lots of people. And there are more now. You're famous. Newspapers sent reporters that are now camped out in our parking lot."

"Why?"

"Because you're the woods spirit, the woman who talks to trees, and then they answer."

"I don't – "

She waved aside my protest. "I know that and you know that, but those reporters smell a story, and they don't care about the truth." Her expression turned cunning. "But don't worry, sweetie pie, we'll keep them at bay." Then it became even more cunning and I decided that she enjoyed keeping people at bay. "No one will get close to you while I'm around to prevent it."

With which she went on her way to check on her other patients, not that there were many of them because Johns Falls is a small town where no one is quite sure whether our hospital is truly a hospital or merely a very large clinic. It's only one story, which means I could look out my window and see that parking lot and, yes, she was right. There were several strange cars and a couple vans with people lounging around them while keeping an eye on the main door in case anything of interest happened.

The nurse popped in again, seeing where I was looking. "Don't worry sweetie, we have a back door, and when it's time to leave we can make you look like a corpse if need be." She arched her eyes at the reporters. "They won't know a thing."

I thanked her and asked when I could leave. "That'll be for the doctor to say, but if I know my business – and I do – then it'll be soon because you seem getting back to normal very fast. Though of course you'll have to take it easy for a while. Days. Weeks maybe."

"With about a million people in town all looking for

me and driving me nuts? I won't get much rest."

She frowned. "Maybe we can arrange something because, if you can't recuperate in peace, you might not recuperate at all." She breezed out again, popping back long enough to say, "But don't worry, we'll come up with something." Her shoulders straightened. "Because this is Johns Falls, and we take care of our own."

That help happened with a little assistance from Jerry, who had an empty apartment above his pizza place that he offered for as long as it was needed, mentioning that if I was spirited from the hospital to the apartment after hours, preferably in the middle of a moonless night no one would see where I went. He then mentioned that tonight would be a new moon, so moving me now would be good.

That night, thanks to lack of a moon, sunglasses that would do a Hollywood star credit, and a huge coat that covered me almost to my ankles, I was in that apartment and sleeping serenely in a comfortable bed with a breeze coming through the door that opened onto a tiny balcony that I was told was so private that I could be on it without being seen by anyone. Max took Casey because if my dog came with me, he'd need to be walked occasionally, and that walk would clue anyone looking for me as to where I could be found.

That was how I spent the next couple of weeks. Max made sure the cupboard was stocked, and he brought food only after hours when no one would ask who was in the apartment upstairs that was normally empty. Casey came with him during those grocery runs and investigated the entire apartment and finally woofed his approval, though he was somewhat miffed at having to leave when the time came. Only Max's promise of doggie treats and a walk with Snow and Frost got him down the stairs.

Each time Max came, he stayed longer than the time before. The balcony was just large enough for two people and a dog, and we took full advantage of it, especially as the new moon turned into a half moon that spent nights casting a soft, white light over everything. We could see the forest beyond Johns Falls, the treetops silver and the night birds black as they soared above it all. Once we saw a Snowy Owl, huge and silent, hunting in the swath of open land between the forest and the town. So high, so magnificent, until it suddenly changed the slant of its wings and dropped like a rock to feed on some unfortunate creature before returning to reign supreme in the air once more.

"Do you ever fear for your safety in the forest?" Max angled down at me and spoke softly because it was a quiet, whispery kind of night. "Not from an owl, of course, but there are dangers in the forest."

I slumped lower in the cushioned lounge. "Like unexpected logs floating in creeks."

He nodded. "And other dangers, especially when you're alone. Casey is old now, you don't take him with you any longer."

I gave his statement careful consideration because I was, after all, recovering from the kind of dangerous encounter he meant, even though Casey couldn't have saved me if he'd been there. Only Max could. "I've never given it much thought because I feel safe in the forest. As if the trees are surrounding me with an invisible security blanket."

I shrugged against the cushions that were so comfortable as I thought still more about my time in the forest. "But, as people say – and you hear it a lot -- I could be hit by a car crossing a street in my home town. So, in a sense, because I know and respect the forest, I don't fear it any more than I fear that street or that car."

He nodded and took my hand in his, lightly, our arms hanging between the lounge chairs, swinging in rhythm to some unheard music. Maybe the music of the night because there's a kind of rhythm to the movements of the moon and clouds and the living things that inhabit the dark. "Know that I'll always come looking if you don't come home in a reasonable time."

"Thank you." Because there was nothing else to say to such a statement. We were friends. No more, but no less, either, and the fact that I loved him didn't enter into that special relationship that we'd forged over our lifetimes. Couldn't, unless I was willing to risk our friendship by telling him and, thus, changing things, and I wasn't. He was too precious to chance it.

He rose because it was past midnight, and he had to work the next day even if I could sleep till noon. He'd brought my laptop so I could work in the apartment when and if I felt like it. Hollander and Company had let me know that I could work half-time or whatever felt right until I was fully healed. Which is why I work for them. Good company. Nice people. Not pushy.

Our hands separated and he stared down at me for a long time. Then, unexpectedly, before leaving, he stooped down and kissed me and then rose again, speaking in a suddenly hoarse voice. "All the years we've known each other and we've hardly ever kissed. Odd, isn't it? Think about that unusual fact. Then think about us." Before I could react, he was gone.

CHAPTER 24

A few days later I received good news, two pieces of good news, and I couldn't decide which was more important. The first was that I was officially given the all clear health-wise. The second was that there'd been a train derailment in Minneapolis, and every single reporter in Johns Falls had cleared out as soon as they could finish their current cappuccino, jump into their vehicles and tear out of town in search of the derailment story.

Every reporter except Gwen Wooster. She waved them all goodbye with her very large mug and told Jerry to refill it because she wasn't interested in the derailment story. Rather, she explained, she was interested in the most interesting story of all and that was me. Had been me all along, and she'd enjoyed being so astute as to figure that out and write about me. Until her story brought all kinds of problems and guilt took over and turned her into a policewoman, and now she was all about protecting me from the fallout of her success as a reporter, and she wasn't leaving until she was sure her job was done.

Anyway, that's what she told me when I finally ventured downstairs and into Jerry's place and saw her sitting where she had an excellent view of the stairs to the apartment and realized she'd known where I was all along. She smiled a lazy, slow smile and said, "I wondered when you'd come down and join the world." Waved her mug in a salute. "I saw you leave the hospital and followed." Smiled even more. "Didn't tell anyone, of course." Finished her cappuccino in one gulp. "Glad the paparazzi finally left." And put her mug on the table with a satisfying thunk. "Welcome back, woods sprite."

"I'm not a woods sprite." An automatic response.

"You are to me." A mysterious expression crossed her face. Not a smile, not a frown, but deep with understanding and some rare knowledge of the human condition that unerringly brought her to the most interesting places on earth at precisely the best times to be there. "You will always be a woods sprite to me, along with also being my favorite story of all time, and not just because writing about you gave my retirement fund a big boost. Because what you can do is amazing and because you are an interesting and very nice --- person."

I wasn't sure how to take her description of me, so I merely dropped into the chair across from her, and watched Jerry make me a cappuccino without being asked because he knew I'd need one after that little speech. It would be unusually hot and would have a bitter under-taste that would be exactly what I needed. "What's next, Anne?" he asked as he shoved it in my direction.

"I go home and start living my life. My real life, the one without reporters hanging over my fence and curious people stopping me in the middle of the block and without big logs hitting me in the head when I go swimming." The cappuccino was wonderful, and I sipped non-stop until it was half empty, which is saying a lot considering how my tongue puckered. When I put it down and gave a heart-felt sigh, my stomach was warm and the world was once again a wonderful place, made even more so by the sight of Max strolling past and peering in the window and then giving a double-take on seeing me. He backed up until he was even with the door, pushed it open and entered.

"Hi." He looked from Gwen Wooster to Jerry to me, unsure what was going on and how to behave. Seeing my steaming mug, he took his cue from that and found his own mug from those on the wall shelf, and soon Jerry was making him a much sweeter drink than mine because Max was smiling from ear to ear, laid-back and as relaxed as possible after brushing a few doggie hairs from his shirt. I inspected them as they floated to the floor. Not white or gray, they were brown and thus were proof that Casey had had sufficient hugs while away from me.

"Casey can come home now." I missed my dog. Missed my life, but starting today it would return to normal. About time.

"I'll bring him around this afternoon." He leaned back, tipping his chair and gazing at the ceiling with a secret smile that disappeared almost as soon as it appeared which meant that he hadn't meant it to be seen because he was hiding something. Something nice by his expression, but I didn't ask because Max outrivals the sphinx as far as secrets are concerned. But as I remained silent, I knew that eventually I'd find out what it was. Because Max can be secretive but I can get anything out of him. It may take a while, but it happens, and I wanted to know what was behind that peculiar expression.

He finished his cappuccino and started to say something, but then stopped as the door to Jerry's opened and a flock of youngish people swarmed inside. The women wore filmy dresses topped by swimmy scarves, and the men wore flashy shirts beneath cowboy hats, and every one of them wore clunky boots. They were young, earnest, and self-conscious, and they gave out such heavy outdoor vibes that I wondered if they knew how to behave in a building. And they searched the room for a table that would hold them all.

After a moment of searching and milling about aimlessly, they dropped into chairs around the only large table in the place that happened to be smack in front of the plate-glass window that gave every passer-by a good look at them, and then they sat, obviously wishing not to be on stage but seeing no way around it. I figured that anyone dressed like that got a lot of attention, and maybe they were tired of it.

Jerry, with one eyebrow raised in either humor or consternation, approached and politely asked if he could help. The de-facto leader, a tallish man with dark, bushy hair and a beard, spoke for them all. "Pizzas, please. Lots of pizzas."

Jerry nodded and waited, because it was obvious that pizza was just the beginning of whatever had brought them to his place. "And pop of course. Or coffee. Whatever you have." Said in a very polite voice, which allowed Jerry to relax because you never know what people will be like, and this group wasn't your usual bunch of tourists.

They settled on pop, and soon he brought several pitchers that they divided among themselves as they settled back to wait for their pizza. And Max and Gwen Wooster and I watched in a kind of awe because their presence enveloped the entire place. We three faded into the background even though they didn't seem to be trying in any way to be obvious. In fact, they seemed to be doing their best to be as inconspicuous as possible while wearing rainbows and cowboy regalia.

As they waited for their pizza quietly, hunching over their pop, they took still more surreptitious looks around.

And saw me.

Their eyes widened. They glanced at each other and nodded. Then they went silent for a moment before their leader, taking a deep breath, rose and came to our table.

"You're Anna Reilly." Nothing for it, he knew who I was, so I nodded and waited for whatever was about to happen because obviously something was. "You're that woman everyone talks about." He held his hat in his hand almost reverently. "The dryad. The woods nymph." I squirmed and wanted to tell them that they had the wrong woman, but these people clearly knew who I was as he continued. "The woman who converses with trees."

Gwen Wooster caught my gaze and her eyebrows lifted saying as clearly as words what we'd all assumed. That more crazies looking for me were now in town in spite of the train derailment. Max blew out of his nostrils as he thought how to handle this new problem, and I forgot to wonder about his secret as the motley crew now staring at us sent everything else from our minds.

The leader stared at me, and his people followed his lead with slightly awed expressions that made me feel like an idiot. I wished I was anywhere but in Jerrys, but that wasn't possible, and all I could do was brace myself for whatever was about to happen.

At which moment Gwen Wooster winked at me, dropped her empty mug casually on the table, and rose, moving just enough to stick her face into the leader's face while blocking me from his sight.

She looked him up and down. "I love the clothes." She pretended to examine their apparel as she frowned just enough to let them know that a question was forthcoming. "But I don't quite get your vibe." She tilted her head. "What are you people about? Love? Peace? Rainbows?"

He took the bait. "Nature." Moving proudly so she could better see his outfit.

"Oh. Nature. Of course," she said in the exact tone she'd used when she first spoke to me over my back-yard fence when she'd wanted to interview me. To nail me to a wall. "You're about the natural world. The colors, the beauty of it all. It's obvious." She waved her hands in the air. "How could I not see it?"

The group looked at each other, proud of what they believed in, but thrown slightly off-kilter by Gwen Wooster's words, which I sure was what she wanted. What she knew would happen. Remembering that day over the back fence, I knew she had a plan, I just didn't know what it was. More importantly, I didn't know if I was included. I hoped not.

She stepped even closer and grabbed his shirt gently. It was a dozen shades of tie-died green with swishes of purple here and there. She pulled him close and spoke earnestly. At least she sounded earnest. I knew that Gwen Wooster wasn't capable of being serious about anything but these people didn't know that. "I'd love to learn about you. Your connection to nature. Your goals. How you live. Everything."

The leader stood a bit straighter. Silently conferred with his flock around the huge table. Then he kind of wiggled around Gwen Wooster until he could see me once more. "We came to see her. The dryad. The woods nymph. The wilderness wizard."

"Her?" Gwen flipped one shoulder in distain and somehow managed to turn him away from me while winking at my little group as she propelled him back to his friends. "She's ---" She pretended to search for the right word. "Competent." She shrugged. "That's a good thing but that's all she is. A competent forester."

He was confused. "She found that little boy when no one else could."

"Because she grew up around here." She subtly pushed him into a chair and towered over him. "So, of course she found him. Probably checked the places she played when she was a kid and there he was." She shrugged again as if finding Bobby Deal was no big thing. "Anyone from around here could have done the same thing. She just happened to be the one who did."

The pizzas arrived, and the group forgot all about dryads and wood nymphs as they dug into pepperoni and sausage. Gwen Wooster, observing them from her considerable height, nodded, and I knew that whatever she was doing was going as planned. She grabbed a slice of pepperoni and, as she stuffed it in her mouth, spoke so casually that I knew she'd thought precisely what to say. "But you guys, now, unlike Anna Reilly, you are the real thing. The real deal. True children of nature. Dryads."

They stopped. Sat a little straighter. A couple of the women dipped their heads and touched their long, flowing hair, as one of the men rolled his sleeves a bit higher, exposing tanned, muscular arms. Whoever these people were, they spent a lot of time out-of-doors, and they worked hard. But all their leader said was, "We try. We want to save the earth."

The man with rolled-up sleeves continued. "We work hard. We learn. We are dedicated to living a pure life in nature."

Gwen Wooster's hands went up in a half-prayer. She could pass for a religious icon. "Wonderful! Amazing! Most people today can't be bothered. They won't get their hands dirty."

"We do," the leader said ruefully, putting his hands out in front of him for all to see. "Real dirty." They were grimy and had broken nails.

Gwen Wooster took one of those hands between hers and stroked it. "They are beautiful. I'd love to know how these hands got this way." She looked him in the eye. "Weathered. Worn. The hands of someone who knows how to live with nature."

It was a subtle thing, the change in the entire group, but we three in the back of the room saw it happen. We saw Gwen Wooster swing those people's thoughts from me to their lifestyle as she continued. "Would you tell me how you do it?" They were confused. "Will you show me? Teach me? Please."

"What could we teach you?" They looked from one to another.

Those long, skinny arms that had topped my backyard fence waved elegantly. "Everything. Nature. Hard work. The great outdoors. Whatever it is that you people are doing that's so intriguing that just seeing you today makes me want to learn all about it." They looked at each other without speaking, so she added, "And when I learn what you do and how you do it, I want to tell the world."

"We want to make the world a better place."

"Well I'm a reporter and a good one, so tell you what. You do the teaching. I'll do the telling, and the world will be better for it. Deal?" She held out a hand and, slowly, the leader took it.

With which the entire group, acting as one person, accepted Gwen Wooster into their midst, making room for her at the table and talking over each other in their eagerness to explain who they were and why they were walking around in ridiculous, colorful clothes and getting their hands dirty. Gwen Wooster listened intently and only once threw a glance my way that gleamed with the humor of the situation, as she promised to share their secrets with the world if they'd let her follow them around for a few days.

Which could happen. She'd followed me, and the result had gone all over the world.

When they finished their pizzas and rose, Gwen Wooster rose with them. On her way out, she grabbed her mug and let that gesture tell us that she was taking it with her because she'd not be back because she was on her way to another story.

As she sashayed towards the door, she managed to side-track enough to come by our table. She whispered. "I promised to protect you from the paparazzi, even if they are disguised as rainbows, and I keep my promises." She patted me on the shoulder. "Besides which, this group just might prove to be as good for my career as you've been. Another hole in one, so to speak. I'll be rich yet." She waved as she left. "Goodbye, little dryad, and it's been interesting."

CHAPTER 25

So once more my life became as normal as possible considering that it had been turned upside down and that in the midst of that turmoil, I'd discovered that I was in love with Max and would have to live the rest of my life loving him and wishing that he loved me. Which he didn't because he was just Max, the childhood friend who would always have my back but who would keep his heart to himself.

I worked for Hollander and Company a lot. I stared at my computer and wanted to throw it across the room, but I didn't because it belonged to them. I went for a lot of walks. Once I would have taken Casey, but he was getting old and preferred lying in the heat of the back yard where he could bake until his fur smelled like sun. So I went alone into the forest that had always given me solace.

Not deep into the woods, because I was too restless to disappear, as I'd done other times. Just enough to know that, for some reason, the forest no longer gave me the peace I thought it should. That it normally gave me. I took short jaunts, frowning because I was honest enough to admit why that was so, but it was hard to come to terms with being in love with someone who'd never love me back because he was too busy being a friend.

So I pushed through the thick underbrush that's the edge of the woods, the part where the sun and rain hit and ragged bushes grow wild. Snorting, angry with myself, and wondering when this ennui would end and I'd be a real human again.

A sound behind me stopped me in my tracks.

"No dog?" I turned to find Max studying me, Snow and Frost by his side. "How many times have I told you that you shouldn't be in the woods without a dog?" I explained about Casey. "Take Snow or Frost. Or both of them. Be safe. They'll know if there's something nearby that wants to hurt you. Or eat you."

I stared at him, unsure whether to wish him gone or with me, because I wanted both and neither. This being-in-love thing was ridiculous. I was losing my mind. I'd just better take myself in hand and figure out how to handle me if I was to get on with life.

I opened my mouth to tell him that I wanted solitude and, instead, melted when he said, "Or we could go for a walk together, and the dogs can come with us." He moved closer but something, my expression probably, as if I wanted to bite someone and he was available, kept him from coming too close. He backed up a bit and sort of squinted to read me better. "If you want to, that is. If you're not looking for solitude."

"No solitude." The words came unbidden before I knew I was going to speak or what I would say. "You know that I'm a people person." He rolled his eyes at the obvious lie but didn't laugh, and for that I was grateful. "I'd love company. You and the dogs."

I turned to lead the way into the woods, and Max caught up, and we struck out for the deep forest with the dogs loping alongside us, and I knew that this impromptu trek would be good for me. Mac and me together was what had been missing before he arrived and was what I'd wanted all along, no matter that we were friends instead of lovers.

We didn't discuss a route, we just walked. At least that's what I thought we were doing until somehow, we veered towards the creek with the small pond where we'd gone swimming, and I'd been knocked unconscious. "Nice place," Max said casually as it became obvious where we'd end up. "Clean, warm water." I snorted. "Big logs don't come along often." I giggled, and he continued. "If we go swimming, I promise to keep watch."

He touched my hand to slow me down. Just touched me and I felt it through my whole body. I gathered my resolve as I realized that a platonic relationship would be hard. It would take practice and fortitude to survive the rest of my life. The only thing keeping me from running screaming was acknowledging that friendship was better than nothing.

So we arrived at the pond, and Max slid the backpack I'd not paid attention to from his back and brought out a bright tablecloth that he spread on the ground, to which he added an assortment of picnic-like snacks. Some Little Debbie cakes, potato chips, the remains of a bag of chocolate chip cookies, and several flavors of pop. My mouth dropped open. "You planned this!"

A self-satisfied expression was his answer, but he grudgingly said, "Good planning would have included decent food, but I found a few things."

There was only one explanation that made sense and still kept our friendship intact. "Is this an intervention? Bringing me to the scene of the crime, so to speak, so I'll not be afraid to come again?"

A surprised expression said that wasn't his reason, as he lowered himself to the cloth and chose a snack cake. "I like this place. I have fond memories."

"You have fond memories of me being knocked in the head by a log?" Really?!

He leaned back on his elbows and examined me. "I'm thinking of a different memory. A nice one."

It had been good day until the log came along. The sun beaming into the tiny piece of open sky. The shallow pond. The cool, clear water.

Then it hit me. What he was talking about. His fond memory. I'd rambled on while out of my head, and whatever I'd said was now making him smile.

What had I said that now had him almost laughing? No, not laughing exactly, but he was enjoying himself. I took a deep breath and said in a strangled voice, "Tell me what I said, and when you answer please remember that I wasn't normal when I said it."

He was unperturbed. "I'm fairly sure you'd never have said it if you'd been thinking straight." Then he said something that made no sense. "Neither of us would have said what we said then so it's good that log knocked inhibitions out of us both."

Oh dear.

"What did I say? Tell me." I braced myself for whatever horrible, terrible thing I'd said that proved what an idiot I am.

Before answering, he pulled me down beside him

and then so close that I could smell the sun on him and the low, musty scent of my beloved forest. The combination was lethal, and I tried to pull back, but his arm that had come around me kept me fast. Not a hard embrace, nothing scary, just making sure I was where he wanted me.

"You said you loved me."

My breath went out in a rush. What to do now? How to convince him my words weren't true so we could go on being friends? So I could continue being with him even if not the way I wanted? I thought wildly, coming up with dozens of replies in the space of seconds and rejecting them all just as quickly because he knows me, he'd know I was lying.

Before I figured out the right answer, he continued. "Which was nice because I've been wondering for the last year or so how to tell you that I'm in love with you, and that was the right time, and I said the words, but you don't remember."

If my breath went out before, now I was left with none as his words penetrated, and all I could say was, "Huh?"

We were so close that I could feel his held-back laughter. "That's your response to me telling you that I'm in love with you? Not very flattering."

"I – I – I --." I truly didn't know what to say. Couldn't put together a complete sentence. Just sat in that small clearing with the sun pouring down and his arms around me while I tried to grasp what was happening.

He didn't wait for me to figure it out. He pulled me still closer and turned me around, so we were face to face. Inches apart. Eyeball to eyeball. "So what do you think? Since you love me, and I love you, should we consider doing something about it?"

He released me slightly, and the world came back in focus. The place, the cloth we were sitting on, the snacks he'd brought. He opened a can of pop. "If you want to think about it for a bit, we have sustenance while you're deliberating." He took a swig. "As for me, though, you should know that I know what I want."

My voice was so hoarse I wasn't sure he'd understand. But he did. "And what is that? What do you want?"

"You." The answer was sure and final. "I want you in my life from now until forever."

I cleared my throat. Tried to speak and stopped when all that came out was a croak. Waited a few seconds. Cleared my throat again. And spoke. "That sounds good. It's what I want too. You. In my life. And me. Us, that is. Together." I stopped, because I was making a real mess of things and not making any sense at all.

He didn't see it that way. He saw my incoherent ramblings as a 'yes' and proceeded to bring me close once again, and then we kissed, and as the world sort of melted away and became just Max and me and nothing else, I thought in some obscure corner of my mind how we'd been friends since we were old enough to walk, and how we'd only had a few friend-type kisses before today, and they hadn't meant anything.

This kiss wasn't like that at all. This one counted. Big time.

Then we went wading and finished most of the snacks, but not all because they were overly sweet and we didn't need any more sweetness. Then as the sun's disappearance from that tiny open space overhead told us that the day was passing and we'd tarried long enough, we gathered up the picnic things and went home.

And told everyone we knew that we were engaged, and no one was surprised at all. Jerry merely said that it was about time since we'd been destined to be together ever since we were kids. As he said -- with rolled eyes -- we were the only two people in the world who actually enjoyed spending days on end in the depths of a forest where bears and cougars and other unfriendly things could be found.

He finished his little speech, and I thought about the forest. All the things I loved about it. Wildflowers, though I didn't mention them out loud because only those who love the forest passionately understand and love of those fragile blossoms that hide in cracks and crevices beneath the trees. And butterflies. And lovely, clear ponds for wading. And the pungent smell of earth, and wind, and trees. And more. Everything.

"The wedding will be in Max's yard, of course," Jerry said, sliding a pizza our way because we'd mentioned being over-stuffed with sweets, and Jerry is big on healthy eating, pizza being the healthiest. "Because the forest starts at the edge of his yard."

We looked at each other and knew that was where we'd join our lives.

And we did, a few weeks later, before cold weather made the outside world uncomfortable. I wore a white dress that several people said should have been shades of green to celebrate my status as a world-famous dryad, but they laughed when I threw a can of pop at them, and they admitted that I was lovely in white.

Eventually, everyone left, and Max and I began our life together in that very house because it was his and it was where we wanted to live. With three dogs and the forest close at hand.

THE END

Dear Reader:

I hope you liked this book. If you did, I'll be forever grateful if you'll post a review on Amazon. Simply go to Amazon and type in _The Pathfinder_ by Florence Witkop and then follow the prompts.

You also might like to read some of my other FGMN and TMA books so I've included a bit about each of them below, along with a link to find them on Amazon.

And here's a link to my website in case you want to learn more about my journey as a professional author, about my other books and short stories, or my thoughts on writing fiction. http://www.FlorenceWitkop.com

Blessings and happy reading to you all.

Florence Witkop

ABOUT THE AUTHOR

Florence has been an elementary teacher, an IT person, has owned (with her husband and 5 kids) a family-friendly resort in northern Minnesota, and at present is helping make and sell fudge and fudge-filled treats, a family business she joined after her husband passed that started with the family recipe for Christmas fudge.

Most of all, though, Florence is a writer and has been ever since driving through near-blizzard conditions to the school where she taught first grade while thinking how she'd always intended to become a writer. Being a sensible person, when the school year ended, she said goodbye to teaching, became a full-time, professional writer and has never looked back.

She's been a ghost writer, written confession stories, done editing, written advertising copy, written some non-fiction articles, written literary and science-fiction short stories, written both novellas and novels, and won the only literary contest she ever entered, becoming Minnesota's Region 2 Literary Person of the Year.

She now writes for Winged Publications where she writes for both Forget Me Not Romances and Take Me

Away Books. In this clean and Christian-oriented market, she writes romances peopled with happy, well-adjusted characters who aren't looking for love or adventure but find them anyway, and the path to their happily-ever-after ending keeps readers involved until the very last page.

Check out some of Florence's books:

The Man From Yesterday

http://www.Amazon.com/dp/B07NBL1XFZ   What if you went for a walk and brought home a man from another era? Impossible? Maybe not! When Carey finds an unconscious man among the wildflowers, he awakens knowing only her farm as it was a hundred years ago. He's clearly suffering from amnesia and 'something else' that the doctor doesn't understand. But when the doctor tells Carey that he'll recover his memories faster in familiar surroundings, she offers her home rather than sending him to an institution, not dreaming that he'll become a crucial part of both her business and her heart. But, as his memory returns, they realize the 'something else' is that he's actually from the past. He traveled in time. And may do so again.

Shh – Don't Tell

http://www.amazon.com/dp/B077RMTT2C   Recently jilted, Chloe Brown is back home in Johns Falls, Minnesota, working for her aunt selling furniture and other garden paraphernalia until she can recover emotionally, after which she'll leave. When she discovers a family of Mallard ducks in one of the huge vases in the outdoor portion of the store, her aunt agrees to let them stay because protecting the ducks is taking her niece out of her severe depression. Soon Chloe meets Ryan, short-term, interim manager of the Johns Falls newspaper. The two agree to support each other during this temporary, small-town stage of their lives, after which they will happily leave Johns Falls and each other. They find themselves sharing confidences, but Chloe has sworn to protect the duck family and keep them safe, so she keeps their existence a secret lest Ryan write about them in the paper, because a story could bring unwanted publicity, too many visitors, and possibly danger. But secrets have a way of being uncovered, especially by experienced reporters. And love isn't temporary.

A Very Black Cat

http://www.amazon.com/dp/B07BTGN58M   Becky is a dedicated small-town career girl following her pre-determined course to be the best bookkeeper in the area and now, with the blessings of her boss and all-around nice guy Tobias Whittaker, she'll also be a genuine business consultant with a framed diploma on the wall as soon as she finishes an online course that she'll fail without help from someone who understands the nuances of the people side of small town businesses. Enter Jackson, hunky, former football jock and newish, charismatic owner of the lumberyard in town whose charm can convince the must obstinate customer to buy something, whether that customer knew he wanted it or not, and whose boyish smile can subdue even the most stubborn heart, but who can't keep his books straight no matter how hard he tries.

Add one small, black cat with a mind of its own into the mix that's not about to watch his two favorite people live without each other one second longer than necessary. Then, along with the entire town of Johns Falls, Minnesota, sit back and enjoy the action.

The Christmas House

http://www.Amazon.com/dp/B07H1ZYMSP   *More than anything, Abby Carr wants to own the house in the forest where she spent many happy, childhood summers and she can have it if she follows the rules her grandmother laid out for owning it. Having quit her job and moved to the north woods of Minnesota to live there and eventually own the house in the forest, she moves in -- and realizes her grandmother wasn't specific about the requirements. Exactly what does 'living the old way' mean? And how can she 'make a living and become a permanent resident' when she can't find a job? But she'll do her best. Until, on her very first day she gets between a mother bear and its cubs and barely escapes with her life. Things go downhill from there and only the help of her hunky neighbor promises to get her through the year alive and undamaged. Bruce Merriweather grew up in the wilderness and pretty much knows everything there is to know about living in the forest and is willing to tutor Abby if she'll pay for the lessons with her to-die-for muffins, which he dearly loves. Muffins? Really? With no other options, she agrees, ignoring his effect on her libido because both of them are too busy surviving in the forest to have time for romance. But romance has a way of sneaking into any and all hearts and Christmas in the forest is the perfect time and place for love.*

Spirit Legend

http://www.Amazon.com/dp/B077TT5V53 Charlie, forester, guides her boss and the owner of Macallister Outdoors to a tiny lake in the middle of a wilderness tract he recently purchased so he can see with his own eyes the spirit that legend says lives there and uncover the truth about it. Suddenly, a rogue storm destroys the dam that created the lake, the surrounding forest, and much of their equipment. They are stranded. Then they see the spirit and hear it sing. It's real, it's beautiful, and, not knowing if it's friendly or not, they fear that it will die when the lake drains dry so they take a chance and begin patching the dam while deliberately ignoring the growing attraction between them because a romance between boss and employee is always a bad thing. But some spirits can do more than just sing. And romance has a way of developing even when it's not wanted.

Wolf Legend

http://www.amazon.com/dp/B077WCSBB3 Jane, who dislikes wolves because they kill her livestock, takes Buck Portman, wolf researcher and wildlife professor at a nearby college she attends, to an island to seek out the huge wolves of legend … the dire wolves of prehistoric times … that local fishermen say they've seen there. She's skeptical until a huge wolf runs through their camp and mentally connects with Jane and invites her to visit so they can sort out this strange mental phenomenon that neither of them expected. Jane follows the wolf and Buck follows her into another world, another dimension, one populated by larger-than-life dangerous animals, including the wolves of legend. Her mental connection to the alpha wolf is all that keeps them alive in this dangerous world and when they return, at the request of the alpha female, they take with them an injured wolf pup to be healed. The pup heals nicely… but as it grows, will it remain a pet or will it become a dangerous predator in a world where it doesn't belong? As the attraction between Jane and the professor grows, so do the problems inherent in having a huge, prehistoric wolf in today's world.

Earth Legend

http://www.amazon.com/dp/B077Y37FB8 Elle Olmstead isn't your normal, every-day botanist. She's different. As a descendant of Ceres, goddess of the harvest and fertility, she, like others of her family, has a magic touch with plants. Real, honest-to-goodness magic. Which is why she unwillingly stows away on the Destiny, a space ship filled with ten thousand colonists heading for a distant planet. Because she knows that her abilities are essential to keep the plants alive that keep the colonists alive and that will be the basis for their survival when they reach their destination. She's caught and thrown in prison, where her powers are useless. Soon the plants begin to shrivel and die. Starvation is imminent, not to mention that the plants provide essential oxygen. But no one believes her when she tells them who she is and what she can do, especially not Cullen Vail, the one person she has come to like, maybe even love. Because Cullen is head of Security, an inscrutable, military type who has no time for stowaways and doesn't believe in foolish legends. She lied to get on board, why should he believe her now? But somehow, she must persuade him of the truth or ten thousand people will die.